Deceptions

A Raven Micheals Mystery

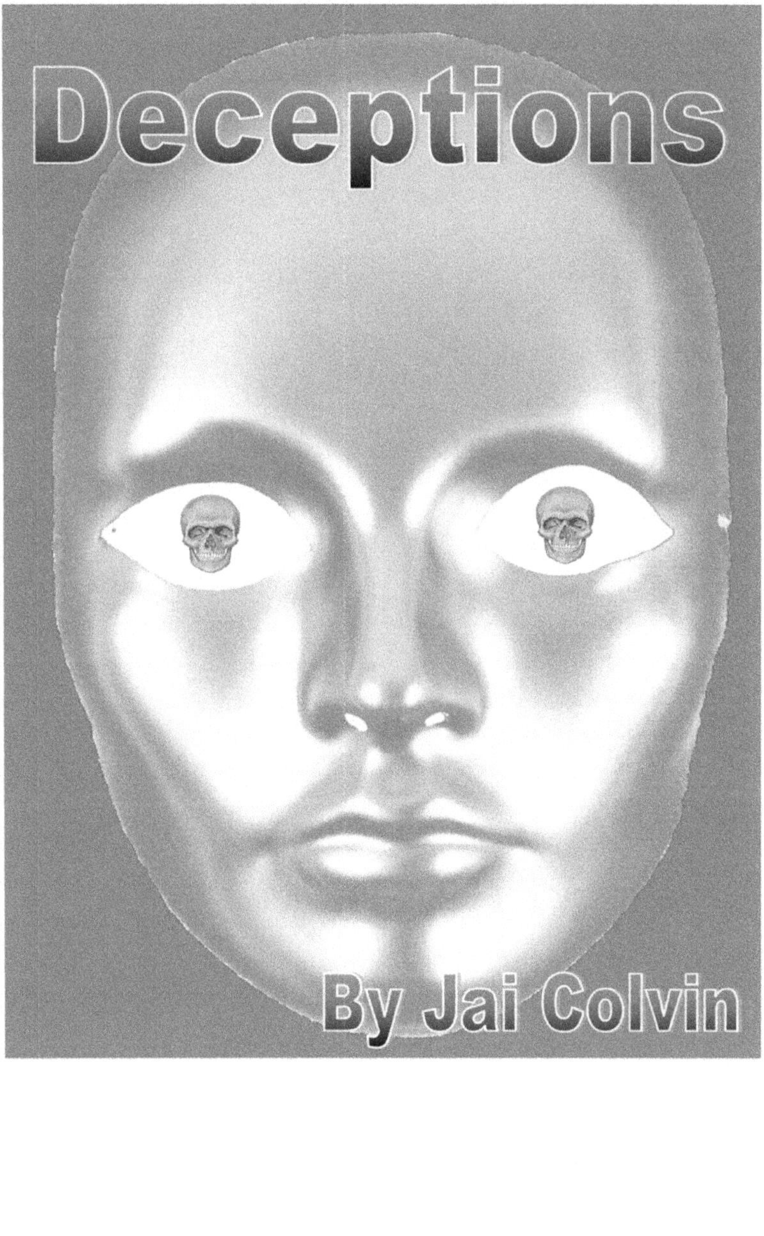

By Jai Colvin

Table of Contents

JAI CALVIN

Deceptions

Re.ad Publishing, Inc.

DECEPTIONS

Published in the United States by Re.ad Publishing/July, 2015
First published by Denlinger's Den in 2002, ISBN 0-87714-800-7

Re.ad Publishing, Inc.
145 Corte Madera Town Center, Suite 437
Corte Madera, CA 94925
Visit our website at www.readpublishing.com

Acquisitions Editor: Amanda Barnett

ISBN 978-1-63160-105-7, print
ISBN 978-1-63160-497-3, ebook

For Aaron Kasper, Ryan Kasper, Jordan Colvin & Jessa Colvin, a person couldn't ask for better kids.
One dragon at a time, guys.

Chapter 1

"Married? You're actually going to get married?" Johni threw up her hands and walked to the service bar she'd just had installed in the den just last week; now was as good a time as any to try it out. She poured a scotch, neat, and sat down hard on one of the four custom made bar stools she'd had imported from Italy. She couldn't believe that after knowing a woman only two months Ricki, her best friend, would even be considering marriage. What the hell was she thinking?

Johni didn't have a great many people in her life she cared to call a close friend and Ricki was as close as they came. As a successful novelist she found that there weren't a lot of people she could trust; with money and fame came a price. Ricki had become one of the chosen few to make Johni's very short list. They shared a history; they had gone to high school together, served in the military together, were both born and raised in the Pacific Northwest; they were family. Then there was the fact that Ricki had played perhaps her most important role by introducing her to Raven Michaels, Johni's one and only true love. The introduction to Raven was something Johni could never pay back. When it was all said and done Ricki was more family than friend despite her hundreds of annoying traits. There was a connection that could not be broken, nor explained, which, in Johni's mind, gave her every right to be both appalled and irritated that her friend would be considering marriage to a woman she barely knew.

When Ricki had called earlier in the evening to announce that she would be dropping by, she insisted that both Raven and Johni be there because she had earth shattering news that "just couldn't wait". When they got the call, she or Raven were moved by the possibilities that Ricki's announcement held; Ricki's whole life was full of "earth shattering news" whether it was a new make money quick scheme or some woman she had just met that was "the one". This was a regular Friday night in Ricki's world which was why Johni had protested giving up their evening at first, but Raven told Ricki to come on up anyway.

One of the nice things about living up on Reman's Hill was that visitors had to call. There were no, "just in the neighborhood excuses" possible. One always had to call or run the risk of finding an empty Wind Shadow, the 4200 sq. ft. home Johni had built Raven. It sat perched on the very spot where they had first given into their love for one another. It was their sanctuary.

When Ricki had arrived they went into the den and opened a bottle of wine after which Ricki dropped her bombshell on them. Johni's reaction had been swift and decisive...this was a bad idea. She drained the scotch and poured herself another while Ricki explained her crazy plans to marry a woman she'd just met. Johni snuck a glance at Raven and was not surprised to see her trying to be supportive.

"You can't marry someone you barely know Ricki, that's nuts," Johni restated as she plopped down on the sofa. "What if she's an ax murderer?"

"Oh Johni you're so morbid. Stop." Raven laughed. She'd been sitting at the bar but now she gracefully slid off the bar stool and stood facing them both. Despite her annoyance with Ricki, Johni had to smile. Raven was a beauty. She stood all of 5'2 and had a well-toned build. She'd been working out a lot lately downstairs in the gym and it was showing. Johni had it put in for Raven's birthday, doubtful at first that she would actually use it and then pleasantly surprised when not only did she use it but she did so every day. Someone who didn't know her would never have guessed she was 40 years old. Raven caught Johni looking, smiled and winked. Johni adjusted on the couch in order to keep the tingling in her stomach controlled. Pathetic, Johni thought to herself, all she did was wink. Raven focused her attention on Ricki who was just beaming. Johni could see that talking her out of this one might be harder than normal.

"Do you love her?" Raven asked point blank.

"Yes." Ricki answered without hesitation.

"What do you know about her?"

"Well, the basics," Ricki started. Raven held up a hand.

"Really know, Ricki."

"Like what?" Ricki asked, slight annoyance in her voice. It was becoming apparent that Ricki had hoped that she and Raven would just be overjoyed and give her their blessings. She really should have known better.

They themselves had only met the woman once and, to be honest, they had not been that impressed.

"Like who are her people? Where was she born? Does she leave the cap off the toothpaste?" Raven asked folding her arms across her chest. Uh oh, Johni thought, she's ready for battle. Ricki took a deep breath and then let out a long exasperated sigh.

"Raven, I know the things that I need to know right now. All the other stuff I'll learn as I go. I love her, does that count?" Ricki started to pout. "You guys are my best friends, don't let me down by trying to throw a wrench into my plans. I love her Raven, I really do." Ricki was pleading and Raven did something that Johni didn't see her do very often, she dropped her arms. She was backing off.

"Are you sure Ricki?" Johni searched Raven's face for some reasoning as to why she was letting this go so easily; nothing, just concern. "She's nice, I agree, but I just wouldn't want you to get involved with anyone who would hurt you." Ricki smiled and hugged Raven.

"I know Raven and I appreciate that but she's a wonderful person and she loves me too." Raven hugged Ricki back. Over Ricki's shoulder she gave Johni an exasperated look.

"That's great Ricki. Then if you're happy, we're happy." Johni made a noise that sounded distinctly like humph. Raven shot her a look and Johni smiled. "We are both happy for you, isn't that right honey," The way Raven said it wasn't a question so much as it was a statement. Johni knew the tone and that it could be detrimental to disagree at this point so she sucked it up and decided that they would discuss it further after Ricki was gone.

"Yeah, sure Rick, that's great." Johni got up and fixed herself another drink; she was going to need it to get through the fibbing she was doing. She tuned Raven and Ricki out as she poured the drink. They were discussing plans and a wedding and all the crap that follows it. She really hated doing the plans thing and she was especially not interested in helping plan something she didn't believe should be happening in the first place. Raven, on the other hand, loved it. Give her an occasion and she was up for the challenge. She sat down on a stool and watched Raven and Ricki talk. She couldn't shake the initial creepy feeling she had gotten when Ricki announced this crazy marriage thing.

The woman Ricki was talking about marrying was Whitney Rodgers. Johni and Raven first met her at a small dinner party she and Ricki threw not long after they had first met. Ricki had not been a woman of many partners and, in fact, had been with her former girlfriend, Roz, for over 9 years. It had been a surprise when Roz had come home one weekend and announced that she was leaving Ricki for a guy. It didn't happen often in their world but every now and then a woman just jumped back to the other side. It had affected Ricki in a way Johni had never seen coming. She spent the next several months partying it up, laying it on thick with women and generally being wildly irresponsible. Johni had let it go on for as long as she dared and then, one Sunday afternoon, had sat Ricki down and convinced her that this was no way to live. The very next weekend Ricki introduced them to Whitney.

Whitney seemed nice enough at first but then, as that first night wore on, there were little things about her that had come to light. For starters, she watched everyone like a hawk; as if she didn't trust anyone. Usually if a person doesn't trust anyone else it's because they themselves can't be trusted. Johni also noticed how the woman had sat back listening to everyone. It's a writer's occupational hazard to watch everything around them; it's how we do our research and watching Whitney that night conveyed a different story than Whitney herself was telling. At first it seemed as though she might be shy in front of people she didn't know but, when Johni had gone into the kitchen for another beer, Whitney had cornered her and made it all too clear that she was far from shy. Johni had handled it and politely begged off explaining that a woman whom Whitney could not have held a candle to otherwise occupied her. Whitney had smiled and whispered that she'd change Johni's mind before too long. It had been annoying and she toyed with the idea that night of going back to the table and announcing to everyone, Ricki included, that Whitney was a ho. Instead she got the beer and made her way back to the table not telling anyone anything figuring that this thing between Whitney and Ricki was just a passing fancy. She wondered now if she should have at least mentioned it to Raven. She decided to tell her later after Ricki left. One thing was for sure, Whitney Rodgers was not exactly princess charming...that much was obvious.

"So what do you think hon?" Raven was asking. Johni had no idea what they'd been talking about. She was tempted to try and fake her way through but after seeing the skeptical look on Raven's face, she decided to just fess up.

"I wasn't paying attention. What do I think about what?"

"Guam?"

"It's a nice place," Johni answered with a smile. She was sure that wasn't the question. Raven laughed and threw a pillow off the couch at her.

"No not what do you think about Guam, what do you think about going to Guam? For Ricki's wedding." Johni considered for a moment. On the one hand she loved Guam but on the other....

"All the way to Guam?" Johni asked looking at Ricki, "Why Guam? Why not Hawaii?"

"Hawaii is too commercial. Besides, we had some great times there while we were stationed at Anderson," Ricki answered. "The government on Guam is doing the same thing that Hawaii is. They are recognizing gay marriages and trying to draw gay couples to the island to get married. What better place? We will be getting married on a beautiful tropical island and furthering Gay and Lesbian rights as well, "Ricki added with pride. Johni had to admit she had really enjoyed being on the tropical island. They'd been stationed there together when they were first in the Air Force; aw to be young and stupid again. Johni had spent four years at Anderson Air Force Base and Ricki had stayed five; she'd pulled an extra fifteen months and Johni had been envious. They had been in their 20's and the drinking age on the island was 18. Cheap alcohol, young party animals, a tropical island where the water was always like bath water...who wouldn't have loved it. And the women...all those lonely Air Force wives just waiting to see how the other half lived...it had been a blast. She had wanted to return someday and she was sure Raven would love it. She made up her mind, despite her objections to Ricki's impending marriage, that Guam would be fun.

"I guess we could. It would be a nice trip," Johni answered. "I just finished the new novel and sent it to the publishers and we had planned to take some time off. Yeah we can do that." Raven beamed. Johni was pretty sure that the smile in her eyes was more for all the wedding planning than for the tropical vacation but that was okay.

"Great, then it's done," she said hopping up. "I'll make the travel plans for Johni and I tomorrow and we'll meet you there."

"Tomorrow?" Johni was in the middle of taking a drink and almost choked.

"Tomorrow," Raven confirmed. "Ricki and Whitney are leaving in the morning."¶

"Kind of short notice isn't it?"

"It was a gift from Whitney," Ricki bragged. "She surprised me with the tickets yesterday."

"There's no problem is there," Raven asked walking over to the bar. Johni could tell by the sound in her voice that Raven really wanted to go and that she had better not say that there was a problem. She walked over and gathered Raven up in her arms.

"No," Johni smiled pulling her close and kissing her nose. "We can go."

"Great!" Raven said hugging Johni's neck. Johni laughed.

"I guess we'll see you in Guam Rick." Johni offered her hand to her friend who took it and pumped it hard.

"Thanks Johni," She said smiling. "I'd better get. Whitney's waiting for me at home and we still have some packing to do." They saw Ricki to the door and when she was gone Raven turned and hugged Johni again.

"This is going to be so much fun," she whispered in Johni's ear.

"Oh yeah? And just what do you have planned?"

"Well I've always had this fantasy..." Raven let her words trail off seductively. Johni scooped her up into her arms and headed for the stairs.

"Yeah? Tell me about it," she said as she mounted the first step.

"There's a beach involved," Raven whispered into Johni's ear. She felt Raven's warm breath on her ear and instantly had the urge to stop on the stairs and make love to her there; instead she continued up the stairs.

"Aren't there any travel agencies open tonight?"

"No, but we can practice for the beach," Raven

answered, her lips still close to Johni's ear.

"Practice?" Johni said moving a little faster up the stairs, "Yeah I think we need to...lots of practice. You know, just in case there are any tourist and all. Wouldn't want to look like we didn't know what we were doing." Raven nuzzled into Johni's neck.

"Oh baby you don't need to worry about that. You know exactly what you're doing there." At the top of the stairs Johni paused to kiss Raven full on the mouth. Raven marveled at how strong Johni was to be able to hold her in her arms for this long.

"Am I heavy?" Raven baited as they headed into the bedroom.

"You're fishing." Johni said smiling.

"And...."

"No, you're not heavy," Johni answered setting her down on the bed. Raven reached up and pulled Johni down on top of her.

"Good answer," she breathed and kissed Johni deeply.

Chapter 2

Raven reached up carefully for the alarm clock illumination button. In the past she had been known to hit the button, knock the clock off into the floor, and if that didn't wake Johni, all the cussing that followed the seemingly louder than possible crashing of the clock as it hit the floor, did. Johni was sleeping so peacefully she didn't want to wake her so she took extra care reaching for the button this morning. Hitting the button and stretching to see the time, her suspicions were confirmed. It was only 4:20 a.m. She sank back into the pillow and sighed heavily. This was the third day in a row she was wide awake at 4 a.m. or better; it was ridiculous. She didn't normally have trouble sleeping, yet, here she was, in the dark, cussing out the Sandman for having abandon her once more.

She reached over and ran her hand along Johni's peaceful sleeping face. Part of her wanted to shake her awake just so that she wasn't the only person in the room who was becoming so closely acquainted with the early morning hours; but, she didn't, instead she kissed her lightly on the forehead. After the way she and Johni had devoured each other last night she should be tired as hell not wide awake. She smiled as she briefly slipped back in time 5 hours to the frantic way they had made love. Johni had carried her upstairs channeling some romantic leading man from an old black and white film but once they made it upstairs they couldn't help but dive into each other like they had been kept on separate islands for a month. They didn't always fall into frantic lovemaking but from time to time, it just seemed warranted and, she had to admit, it was good to devour and be devoured once in a while.

Sliding carefully from under Johni's arm she got out of bed. As she stood up Johni stirred but didn't wake. After a few moments, satisfied that she hadn't disturbed her, Raven grabbed her robe and quietly crept out of the bedroom, gently closing the door behind her. Once in the hall she let out the breath she'd been holding. She had to smile. A year ago, when she and Johni first moved in together, Johni had been such a light sleeper that if Raven had let that breath go in the room, she would have woken up; it had driven her nuts. She had always been an early riser, although not 4 a.m. early. Because Johni did a lot of late night writing she, on the other hand, almost always slept in. She was forever waking her up as she tried to get out of bed and the guilt that always followed would have made a Catholic blush. Now, a year later, Johni didn't so much as shift positions when she got up. She had gotten used to someone else in the house which was a good thing for both of them. Now, most mornings, she would come downstairs claiming to not have heard a sound when

Raven got up. She glanced once more at the closed bedroom door and headed downstairs.

Raven took the stairs slowly relishing in the silence of their home. Johni had this house built for them. She had commissioned an architect and she and Raven had laid out the plans together. Their home was built to their exact specifications and it was gorgeous. Johni had followed every detail down to the five hundred bottle wine cellar below. The house had a flowing entryway with marble floors that lead into a large living room which Raven had decorated with the most regal European antiques she could find; several pieces they had even flown to England to buy themselves. Once in the living room, to the left, one could take the five steps up to into the kitchen, which was furnished with an island stove in the middle of the floor coupled with a butchers block on one end as well as all of the latest appliances and cookware, some of which hung carefully above the center island for easy access. Or, you could take the three steps down to the right, just past the staircase, into the study. The study was Johni's domain. She had allowed Raven to decorate it anyway she saw fit and despite her misgivings, the end results had pleased Johni greatly. She had furnished the study in masculine colors, browns and rusts, and had gone out and found just the right desk which she than refinished herself. When she was done the room looked like a writer's study should. It was masculine with the slightest hint of a feminine touch and it housed everything that Johni needed in order to work without interruption. The study was furnished with a half bath so that when she was working Johni didn't have to leave "when nature called", and it even had a small fridge stocked with Lemoncello for those nights when the writing was good enough to be rewarded.

Back up the stairs into the living room, if you crossed the room from the study door you found yourself again stepping three steps down into a technological dream. Johni liked her toys and this room was built especially for just that. The far end of the room housed a fireplace with a built in conversation bar directly in front of it. On the left were Johni's pinball machines, two of them that they had purchased in Atlantic City, New Jersey six months ago, and the other one, a Centipede game, she'd had before they'd gotten together. The entire room was hooked up to a surround sound system that Raven's son had installed for them. In fact, James had wired the entire house with music. Every room had a control box that would control the music level in each individual room. James was quite proud of his work, as were Raven and Johni; they boasted about his system to all of their friends and, as a result, four of them had him put the same sound system into their homes.

A pool table occupied the middle of the den although they rarely played because Johni hated to lose. On the right wall there were two top of the line gaming computers loaded with games for anyone who cared to sit down at one. The computers were her handiwork telecommunications were Raven's specialty. She had a really good time setting those up; it isn't often you get handed a blank check and told that you can do whatever you want. Just off of the den, she had a workshop and office of her own. It was huge with a great deal of storage space for her computer equipment as well as the many craft projects she would find herself knee deep in on any given day. Johni often gave her a hard time about using both halves of her brain, technical for the computer work and creative for all the projects. She joked that one day she would come home to find that Raven had knitted a working computer. There was no TV in the den; those were in the bedrooms, of which there were five, all with fireplaces. The televisions were more for guests than anything; they rarely sat down and watched TV. There was a master bedroom, a bedroom for their granddaughter and one for the grandson. The other two were guest rooms for anyone who came to visit. All of the bedrooms were done in Victorian style except the boys' room; it was done in modern day aircraft. (That was Johni's idea.) The house had three and a half baths and the master bath housed a sauna, a jacuzzi and a two head shower.

Outside in the backyard they had a pool put in and fifty

feet beyond that a tennis court, fully lit for night games. Raven gave the house a sweeping glance of approval and went into the kitchen to make a pot of coffee. Once brewed, she poured herself a cup and went out to sit on the back deck. Of all of the things this house has to offer, the back deck was her favorite place to spend time. The morning air was cool so she tightened her robe and snuggled into one of the deck chairs. The terrace was situated on the corner of the house so that you could look out over the backyard or down over the hill into town. You could also see Puget Sound sprawled out over the horizon. She smiled as she looked down the hill at the sleeping city below. It took her back to another time when she was up here on the hill looking at the lights of the city. That time felt like decades ago. She remembered standing on the Hill and wishing that Johni was standing with her. Little did she know that not only would Johni stand beside her but that she would build their home here. Reman's Hill had been their place from the start. She drifted back to the day when she and Johni, purely by accident, ran into each other here on the hill. Until then neither of them realized the other had known about this sacred spot high above the noise of the world. On that day, each of them had come to think about the other; fate had them in its cross hairs even then. It was befitting that they should live here on the Hill now; this is where they belonged.

An owl flew low over the deck causing her to jump slightly; she laughed at her own fright. She liked living away from town, but they definitely had their share of wild life up here and she had to admit that, at times, it was more than she was comfortable with. Johni, however, loved it. She smiled at the thought of her sleeping peacefully up in their bed snuggled under all of those blankets that she insisted they have. She loved her so much. To think that a little over three and a half years ago they hadn't even known the other had existed; it hardly seemed possible. Now, she didn't know what she'd do if anything ever happened to Johni. Like any couple they had their problems, an argument once in a while, and boy could they argue, two control freaks vying for the upper hand, it was pathetic at times. But overall they had a wonderful relationship. They were best friends as well as lovers. Raven couldn't recall having known anyone else she could spend so much time with and not want to scream at by the end of the day. Couples working at home could get to be a sticky situation but with them it didn't matter; Johni was easy to live with. She spent a lot of time writing but she made sure to also take the time to pamper Raven. She never let it go too long before she did something special just to let her know that she was there. Raven did the same. They worked hard to keep the passion alive in their relationship. At times it wasn't easy, especially when

Johni was being stubborn about something in particular, and she could be extremely stubborn, or when she was writing intensely and she got too involved with the story. She could get pissed off at the drop of a hat when one of her characters wasn't doing what she expected and, at times, that frustration would escape out into the rest of the house. Raven always referred to these moments as Johni's BMS, book menopause syndrome. Johni didn't find that very amusing but understood that she couldn't make excuses for something she clearly knew that she did. She would often force a smile and go back to her desk.

They had a love for each other that surpassed anything Raven had ever experienced before. It was incredible. Even their friends bragged about their relationship. In fact, it was not unusual for a total stranger to approach them and tell them how good they looked together; their love for each other definitely showed. Raven finished her cup of coffee as the sun began to crest the trees and the lights of the town below began to wink out. She got up and went back into the kitchen. The clock on the wall read 6:10 a.m. She could hardly believe she had sat outside that long. It had been so peaceful and a great place to reflect but now it was time to dive into the day; there was so much to do if they were heading out of the country. Now she had to turn her mind to other things. Johni would be waking soon and she had breakfast and travel plans to make. She smiled and took a deep breath. "Guam," she whispered, "ready or not here we come."

Chapter 3

Johni, eyes still closed, reached over for Raven and instead got a hand full of empty pillow. Should have known, she thought to herself. Raven couldn't sleep in if her life depended on it. Smiling, despite the thought that it would have been nice to cuddle this morning, Johni threw the covers back and stretched. The sun was already streaming through the window. She looked around for the time; 9 a.m. It was still early as far as she was concerned. Sitting up, she swung her feet around to the floor. The smell of fresh coffee drifted through the bedroom door. Raven must have decided to let her sleep this morning. She could always tell when she wanted her up early because she would come into the bedroom and make noise. Looking innocent, she would then say something like, "Did I wake you?", all the while knowing damn well she had. Oddly, no matter how tired she was Johni just couldn't get angry with Raven for it. One thing about Raven, she didn't bite her tongue or curb her actions....period and she made no excuses for it. Of course that could be a bad thing or it could be a good thing, depending on where you stood in a given situation and half the time Johni had a hard time deciding which was which. She got off the bed and went in to turn on the shower and then hunted for clothes as the shower water heated. She quickly picked out something to wear having no idea what Raven had planned for today; she chose with the understanding that she might well have to change later. She smiled as she pulled out one of her favorite shirts, a stark white button down; it was one of Raven's favorites as well. She thought about the cute little smile she knew Raven would give her when she saw her in the shirt. She loved that reaction. Going back into the bathroom and stepping into the now hot shower Johni reflected on where she had been just over two years ago; she had all but given up on women. She was living a quiet existence all by herself and she'd thought she had been rather enjoying it too until that fateful night during a party at Ricki's when Raven graceful glided into her life.

Ricki and her ex Lori had goaded her into coming to their big "summer affair". It was the annual party they gave every year during the six years they'd lived together. (Last year Lori had seen fit to sleep with her female boss and her husband during which Ricki had discovered them, in Ricki and Lori's bed. Needless to say Ricki threw Lori out.) After several attempts to "beg out" Johni finally agreed to attend, on the condition that her friends didn't try to fix her up with anyone. That lasted four minutes into the party. Ricki and Lori had spent the better part of two hours introducing her to this person or that person. At about 10 p.m. Johni had decided to quietly slip out of the party, hopefully undetected, when a woman caught her eye. She was taken aback by how beautiful the woman was and how intelligent she looked even from across the room. She was staring when Ricki caught her. She asked about the woman and that's when she heard her name for the first time. Raven Michaels. She'd tried to be calm and cool when introduced to Raven but inside she fell apart. They became instant friends and what ensued after that was an adventure neither of them would soon forget. At the time Raven had a girlfriend although they were well on their way to becoming ex-girlfriends. Neither Raven nor Johni was aware at the time of the price they'd pay for their growing affections. Andi, Raven's then girlfriend, had problems; big problems. Before it was all over Andi had been responsible for an accident that almost took Johni's life and the murder of one of Johni's ex's. When the truth finally came to light it had been Raven who'd figured it all out; Andi had completely gone over the edge. At the trial the judge had ruled Andi incompetent to stand trial and she'd been committed to Lakeside Mental Institution in Overton, three hundred and fifty miles away. In Johni's mind that wasn't far enough away. The fear this crazed woman had instilled in them was almost immeasurable; Johni had written bad characters in her books but this had been the first time she had come face to face with a psycho. In the end their love had prevailed, but neither of them would ever forget how close they'd come to losing the other for good. If she didn't know anything, Johni knew that she and Raven could endure anything together; they had, after all, cheated death.

She finished her shower and turned the water off. As she toweled off she heard music coming from downstairs and had to smile. She dressed quickly and headed out of the room. As she reached the top of the stairs she could hear Raven's voice; she knew she'd find. Padding down the stairs as quietly as she could Johni tip toed through the living room to the doorway of the den. She peered in to find Raven standing by the stereo with the karaoke microphone in her hand. She was singing to a country song and she was obviously lost in the words. She was a wonderful singer and Johni loved to listen to her; she sang with so much feeling. Johni stood there until the song was over and then clapped and whistled loudly. Raven turned around, looking slightly embarrassed.

"You shouldn't do that," Raven said in mock protest. She loved it when Johni listened to her singing and Johni knew it. Always a lady, Johni thought with a smile.

"Can't blame me, your voice is wonderful." Raven smiled and put the mic down. She walked over to Johni and slid her arms around her neck.

"You're so good to me," She cooed in Johni's ear. Johni smiled and hugged her tightly. She was lucky to have such a wonderful woman. After a moment Raven let go and stepped back. She was smiling and Johni knew why.

"I love that shirt on you," she said with an appreciative gleam in her eye. Johni nodded.

"I know, that's why I put it on. You can never resist a little cleavage." Raven laughed.

"I figured as much. Do you want some coffee?" Johni considered for a moment. She had some work to do but a cup of coffee with Raven out on the deck sounded so much more inviting.

"Sure. You going to join me?" Raven smiled as she turned to get the coffee. Having coffee on the deck was sort of morning tradition for them and even though they both loved it they still pretended to make the decision to do so every morning.

"Of course." Johni went out and took a seat on the deck. After a moment Raven reappeared with two streaming mugs and took a seat across from Johni. Johni took her mug and took a careful sip.

"Coffee's good."

"Thanks." Raven answered as she sipped on hers. They were both quiet for a couple of minutes, enjoying the silence together. Johni had never met anybody before with whom she could enjoy the quiet. It was nice. Raven finally cleared her throat.

"We have a few things to do today," she said setting her

mug down. She picked up a yellow legal pad from the side table. Uh oh, Johni thought, she's making lists. Raven must have read the look on her face because she swiped at Johni with the pad and laughed.

"Don't worry it's a small one." Johni laughed too. She loved giving Raven a hard time about her organizational obsessions. They couldn't go on a trip to Canada without six or seven lists, two flow charts and a planner full of suggestions as to what to do while there. She tried not to, bless her heart, but she just couldn't help organizing. She was good at it though and Lord knew Johni wasn't organized...fly by the seat of your pants was her motto.

"Okay boss, what's up?" Johni asked teasing. Raven pretended to pout for the slightest second but then went full steam ahead.

"Well first we need to call the travel agency and get plane tickets. I'd like to get them for today but if we have to wait until tomorrow, we'll just have to wait. We need to pack but I'll pack for you because you know how you are. I figured we could have Jessica look in on things here if that's.........," Johni held up both hands.

"Damn woman, hang on."

"What?" Raven asked slightly annoyed at having been interrupted.

"Don't you think you should slow down a bit," Johni asked with a laugh, "you'd think you were making travel plans for the president." Raven looked perplexed.

"Johni, we have a lot of things to do and the wedding is in three days." Johni reached over and took Raven's hand.

"Okay, I understand that but don't try to kill yourself, okay? This is supposed to be fun," Johni said gently. "Tell you what; give me half your list and I'll help."

"Oh, I was going to do that any way." Raven said. Johni laughed; she should have known.

"Okay, go ahead."

"Thank you," Raven answered. "Now, as I was saying," Johni couldn't help but giggle and Raven glared at her for a moment. "Are you finished now?"

"Yes, I'm sorry." Johni said trying desperately not to smirk.

"Okay then, I'll try to get the tickets this morning. If you can pack your things, I'll come up and round you off later," Raven said looking at her list.

"Are you insinuating that I can't pack for myself," Johni asked. Raven favored her with a woeful glance. "Yeah, yeah, okay." Johni added. She really was horrible at packing for herself. Before Raven came along if she forgot to bring anything on a trip, and she always did, she'd just buy a new one. When Raven saw that she owned four irons and Johni explained why, she started packing for her.

"If you could call Jessica and let her know what we are doing that would be great," Raven continued. "I need to go buy a gift. Oh and call James too. If you don't he will undoubtedly try calling and then worry when he doesn't get us." Johni nodded. Jessica and James were Raven's biological children. James was 26, and Jessica was four years younger. They were wonderful people. Raven and her late husband Walker had done a great job raising them. From what Johni could gather they had been an extremely close family. Although she was gay, Raven had married Walker in her early twenties. It had been a time when being out was not accepted and Raven had still been trying to live the straight life. This of course was compounded by the fact that her husband Walker Davidson had been a wonderful man and he had loved and protected Raven with everything he had. She hated making the decision to leave him in order to be with a woman she'd fallen in love with but they had discussed it and in the end Walker just wanted Raven to be happy. They had remained best friends and even though Raven had relationships with two different women before he died, they had never divorced. He was someone Johni wished she could have met. Raven's voice brought her back.

"Did you hear me," Raven was asking. Johni looked at her and smiled.

"You sure are beautiful," Johni said reaching for her hand.

"Oh no you don't," Raven protested, "You always go

there when you haven't been listening to a word I've said." Johni smiled.

"Oh baby,"

"Don't you oh baby me. What did I say?"

"Raven,"

"Uh-huh, see I knew you weren't listening." Raven feigned hurt.

"Okay, you caught me," Johni admitted, "Now what did you say?" Raven sighed heavily.

"Would you *please* let Mac and Olie know where we are going?" She was trying to sound upset.

"Yes." Johni answered smiling. She got down on her knees in front of Raven's chair. "Forgive me?" She asked taking Raven's right foot in her hands and rubbing it gently. Raven loved having her feet rubbed. She started to relax instantly.

"That's not fair," Raven protested. "I'm mad at you."

"No you're not. You can't stay mad at me," Johni said as she continued to rub Raven's foot.

"Yes I can," She protested half-heartedly. Johni put that foot down and picked up the other rubbing it as well.

"No you can't," Johni repeated with a sly smile. Raven put her head back and closed her eyes sighing happily.

"Okay, you win, you're right," She cooed, relaxing completely. Johni dropped her foot and stood up.

"Okay." Raven's eyes popped open and she hit Johni on

the leg.

"You dog!" Johni laughed and pulled Raven to her feet gathering her up into her arms.

'Yeah and...," she asked as Raven tried to look hurt.

"You're bad," Raven said letting Johni hug her and then finally giving in herself.

"But you love me," Johni said with a grin.

"Yeah, I guess I do." Raven sighed. Johni lifted her face up with a fingertip and kissed her fully on the mouth. Within seconds Raven was taken in by the kiss and they were locked in a passionate moment. Finally it was Johni who stepped back.

"If you want to get to Guam within the next three days we'd better get moving." Raven stepped forward and snuggled into Johni again.

"Are you sure," she asked with a sexy little smile. Johni sighed loudly as she fell apart inside.

"Woman!" Johni said in mock protest. Raven pulled her closer

"You can't fight it so come on," she whispered in Johni's ear. Johni let herself be led into the house and up the stairs. Raven shoved her onto the bed and smiled. "*You couldn't refuse me anyway,*" she added as she climbed on top of Johni. Johni knew she might as well say nothing because she was right. Instead she smiled slyly and pulled Raven in close.

"I could too resist you..."

"I love it when you say that," she whispered in Johni's ear, "it's not true, but I love it when you say it." Johni smiled and got lost in making love to Raven.

Chapter 4

Raven loved planes in that way an 8 year old girl loves them. She hated that rubbery feeling that overtook her stomach when the plane first took off and when it landed but she loved the flight in-between. She loved the roar of the engines and the concept of soaring high above the world. Planes made her feel free. Now, as their plane leveled off over the Pacific Ocean, she exhaled. Next to her, Johni sat grinning.

"What are you grinning about," Raven asked trying to sound annoyed.

"You," Johni answered simply. She had held Raven's hand as the plane had taken off so she knew that Johni was clowning her nervousness.

"Very funny. I'm not scared," Raven protested, "It just makes my stomach feel funny." Johni continued to grin saying nothing. Raven huffed and sat back. She hated it when Johni teased her like that. Johni leaned over and kissed her cheek; it was a peace offering. Raven stared straight ahead for a minute and then turned giving Johni a polite smile. Johni laughed quietly, shaking her head.

"You're really something else, you know that."

"What?" Raven asked feigning confusion. Again Johni laughed and shook her head. She laid her seat back and closed her eyes. Raven just smiled and pulled down the lap table. Johni almost always slept on plane rides. Just like a baby who is lulled to sleep sitting on top of the household dryer, planes had that effect on her. She, on the other hand, always stayed wide awake, even on long flights like this one. Eighteen hours first to Hong Kong and then a connecting flight on to Guam...she was pretty sure she would be awake for the whole ride. She decided to concentrate on the wedding plans as Johni emitted a small snore. She laid out her organizer and began to study their itinerary. They had been lucky enough to snag two first class seats on this flight putting them in Guam with enough time to do everything they needed to do. They had spent yesterday packing and closing the house up; letting everyone know where they were going and then they had driven into the city last night finding a hotel next to the airport for the early morning flight. Johni had suggested they drive in so they could be close and not have to fight traffic. Raven had been really stressing about their schedule until last night at dinner when Johni explained that they actually had an extra day. In going to Guam, she had explained, they would cross the International Date Line so in actuality they would be arriving in Guam, yesterday. The concept had tickled her. This kind of made them time travelers...how cool was that? They were actually going to have two of the same day in one week. It was kind of freaky, but in this instance it was also extremely convenient. It would give Raven an extra day to get set for the wedding. Ricki and Whitney had taken care of all the arrangements for the wedding itself but she had to get herself and Johni together.

Johni had promised her that after the wedding they could stay two more weeks on the island a sort of vacation. She wanted to show Raven the sights and teach her how to snorkel. She looked over at Johni. From the subtle rise and fall of her chest and weirdly polite little snores Raven could tell that she was fast and deeply asleep. She smiled to herself; she wished she could relax like that. A flight attendant came around with glasses of champagne, one of which Raven accepted gratefully. Sipping from the glass, she settled back into her seat. They had been fortunate to get these seats on such short notice. Johni always insisted on first class. She was not going to let Raven, or herself, spend eighteen hours on a plane in coach. Hell, she wouldn't let her spend a thirty minute flight in coach. Johni always insisted that she would be comfortable or she wouldn't go. Johni did tease her about being a snob when she didn't object. She wasn't a snob, she would explain, she just liked what she liked and she liked first class. Johni on the other hand didn't always fly first class; sometimes when first class wasn't available, she settled...she'd have to break her of that. As if she heard Raven's thoughts Johni stirred a little and adjusted slightly in the seat. Raven pushed the attendant button and asked for a pillow and then slid it under Johni's head so that she would be more comfortable. Finally, after a lot of adjusting Raven drained the champagne glass pulled out a book and settled in herself. It was going to be a long flight.

* * *

"This is your Captain speaking. Please fasten your seat belts. We will be landing on the island of Guam in fifteen minutes. We hope you enjoy your stay on the Island. Thank you for flying Pacific Airways." Raven started gathering her things as she poked at Johni who was just stirring from her third nap. Johni sat up just in time to see Raven frantically looking around for anything she may have left; Johni couldn't help but laugh.

"You know if you didn't pack that thing," Johni said indicating the shoulder briefcase Raven was so frantically checking and rechecking, "like you were going to another planet for a few months you wouldn't have to worry so much about what you might have left behind." Raven favored her with a woeful glance.

"I need *all* of this."

"For what? We are supposed to be here to have fun. You packed your work. You cheated," Johni accused. They had agreed before they left not to work while on this trip. In fact it had been Raven who had insisted so Johni had left all of her writing at home... sort of, she did bring her tablet. Johni folded her arms for effect and Raven stopped looking for a minute...she knew that she was busted.

"It's not work," she defended, "I just had a few things to tie up." Johni shook her head to indicate that she was not buying it. "Okay, okay, I'll put it away."

"Good and I don't want to see it out again," Johni warned playfully. Raven smiled at her. She knew that if she had really insisted Johni would let her do the work; that would have hardly been fair though. They finished getting themselves together as the plane started its descent. Raven absently reached over and took Johni's hand. Johni looked up and smiled, squeezing Raven's hand and she held her breath until the plane was on the ground. As they unbuckled their seat belts and stood up it was obvious to Raven that Johni was excited. In fact, she had never seen her quite this excited about anything not having to do with her before. She found herself a little jealous. She glanced around to see if anyone was looking and then, satisfied that they weren't, she took Johni's hand and squeezed it to remind her that she was indeed there. Johni looked at Raven and gave her that smile that always reassured her and squeezed her hand back. Making their way to the exit, Johni made sure that Raven was right there with her. That was one of the many things that Raven appreciated about Johni. She always took care of her. She made it her business to always know where she was. The first thing Raven noticed as she stepped off the plane was that it was brighter. It was so bright, in fact, that it was hurting her eyes. She made her way down the steps, Johni closely behind her, and then stopped to don her sunglasses. Johni did likewise.

"It's bright here." Raven said quietly, once they had broken from the crowd.

"We are closer to the equator," Johni explained, "so we're closer to the sun. It's not only brighter here but the suns' affects are stronger here too. You don't just get sunburned here if you stay out in the sun too long, you get seriously baked and in less time." They made their way inside the airport and to the luggage carrier. This was the part Johni hated and it showed on her face.

"What?" Raven asked as they stood waiting for the carrier to start moving.

"I'm just hoping people don't look at us strangely when I pull almost all the baggage off for you," Johni answered sarcastically. Raven swiped at her.

"I am not that bad," She protested.

"Bad? Woman, you give Imelba Marcos a run for her money and I was here for that too. Hell these people are going to think she's come back!" Johni laughed and despite wanting to hit her again, Raven laughed too. The conveyor started and Johni started pulling bags off. By the time she was done there were fourteen. She stood in the mist of them and cringed.

"Damn it, Raven."

"I needed things," Raven said surveying the bags to make sure they had them all. "Oh stop complaining." The sky porter came with the little push cart and looked at Johni inquisitively.

"They're hers," Johni explained quickly. Raven shot her a dirty look and then proceeded to tell the porter they needed the car rental desk. He pointed it out to them and then waved to another porter to help him with their bags. As they walked to the car rental desk Johni couldn't help but laugh.

"Damn Raven," she said shaking her head. Raven tried to be mad but couldn't; instead she just laughed.

"I'm a woman," she defended, "I have needs." Johni just laughed harder. They rented a car and after their luggage was loaded, they set out for their hotel. Johni had made reservations at the island's most exclusive hotel, The Island Winds. When they pulled into the private entrance Raven was more than pleased, but not surprised. In the two years that they had been together she had realized that Johni would take her to nothing but the best hotels in the world. They had already been to the Waldorf in England and to Enchino's in Mexico. When they had gone to France for Johni's summer writer's conference they had stayed on the French Rivera. Johni simply insisted on nothing but the best and this hotel did nothing short of meeting the very highest of Raven's expectations. The private drive entrance was shrouded in vegetation. Almost immediately on the other side of the entry gate the grounds expanded to the most beautiful open area. It was landscaped to perfection. The road from the front gate to the main hotel building was roughly a mile long and wound along the coast with the most breathtaking view of the island's eastern coastline cliffs. Raven was in awe. As they made the last bend Raven, who had been soaking in the cliffs, heard Johni's sharp intake of breath. Turning back to the road ahead Raven saw the subject of Johni's admiration, The Island Winds Hotel. It was majestically nestled in the cliffs. The mountainous back drop gave the hotel the appearance of having been built into the mountain itself. It looked as though it had been built in the Victorian ages when ladies wore dresses and men fought duels. Raven could hardly breathe for taking in its splendor. Johni stopped the rental just in front of the hotel. As the car idled she took a deep breath.

"Well, what do you think," she asked obviously quite pleased with herself.

"Johni," Raven said reaching for her hand, "it's incredible."

"You think you can stay here for a couple of weeks?"

Raven looked at the hotel then back to the cliffs, then at Johni.

"Stay for a couple of weeks?" She asked, "How about the rest of my life?" Johni laughed and pulled the car into the front drive. A valet scurried to open Raven's door.

"Madam, welcome to The Winds," he said as he took Raven's hand and gently helped her from the car. She graciously bowed her head to him and smiled at Johni over the top of the car. Johni smiled back as she handed the keys to another young man. She came around the car to where Raven was standing and waited. Raven knew that they should go in but she was enjoying the feeling she was having while standing here in front of this grand hotel. She reached over, oblivious to anyone else around, and squeezed Johni's hand.

"Well," Johni said stepping forward, "You want to check in or what?" Raven smiled and followed Johni into the lobby. The lobby was just as grand as the outside. Raven looked around while Johni checked in and got their key. When Johni returned with the key she took Raven's hand and set the key in it.

"My lady," Johni said with a bow, "Welcome to your island paradise." Raven laughed with delight and, despite herself, threw her arms around Johni's neck and hugged her.

Chapter 5

Their room was as beautiful as the hotel was. There was a huge soft feather bed and a Jacuzzi on the private deck. Johni had champagne waiting for them which they shared while standing on the deck admiring the sweeping views of the ocean. It was like a dream. They had both showered and changed clothes; Raven had felt stale after such a long flight, and now they were settling in and relaxing before meeting Ricki and her soon-to-be bride for dinner.

"I need to go unpack," Raven said turning towards the door.

"Really?" Johni knew she was right but they had been really enjoying the champagne and the view.

"Really."

"Ah man." Raven kissed her on the cheek and went inside. She was in the middle of unpacking what Johni referred to as her umpteenth suitcase when she suddenly felt Johni behind her.

"And what do you think you're doing," Raven asked leaning back into Johni's body; she loved the softness of it. Johni wasn't a small woman, and although she wasn't what one would refer to as overweight, she was larger. She often came home from the doctor irritated that they referred to her as overweight but healthy. She wasn't very muscular either but she was solidly built and Raven liked that. She had put on about twenty pounds this year which was great as far as Raven was concerned but Johni was trying to lose the newfound weight. She had lost a great deal of weight during her treatments for Hodgkin's last year and Raven had worked hard to put some of it back on her. Johni was in remission now; they had a lot to be thankful for and as far as Raven was concerned she didn't care how much weight Johni put on, as long as she stayed healthy.

"I'm becoming your horny island girl," Johni answered running both hands down Raven's body. Raven shuddered slightly at her touch. This served to spur Johni on; she continued to nuzzle Raven's neck. Raven moaned and turned to face her. She slid her arms around Johni's neck and favored her with a long, slow, deep kiss. Now it was Johni's turn to moan. Raven pulled back and smiled.

"My horny island girl huh," Raven teased, "Does that mean the natives are restless?"

"Uh-huh," Johni responded picking Raven up and carrying her to the bed. Johni laid her down gently and then stood up. Raven smiled as she watched Johni open her robe and let it drop to the floor. Johni reached out a hand to Raven and pulled her to her feet. Slowly she untied Raven's robe and while kissing her shoulders pulled it off and let it join hers on the floor. They stood next to the bed fondling each other's breasts and kissing each other's neck and shoulders. Raven felt her body heat and then flame into passion. Her body's reaction to Johni was immediate and she felt a familiar throbbing. Johni gently traded places with her so that her back was to the bed. Sitting down, Johni slowly ran her tongue from one nipple to the other and then the length from Raven's chest to her stomach, stopping just shy of her belly button. Raven threw her head back and groaned with pleasure grabbing the sides of Johni's head and wrapping her hair up in her fingers. Johni then pulled Raven down on her so that she was sitting on her lap. Again they indulged themselves in long wet kisses. Raven started to push Johni back onto the bed but Johni stopped her. Instead Johni stood Raven up and then laid her down on the bed. She knelt next to the bed, her head between Raven's legs. Raven looked at her questioning and Johni smiled. Reaching up Johni put her hands on Raven's hips and pulled her gently forward. Realizing what Johni intended Raven inhaled with excitement. Johni pulled Raven down so that she could work her tongue along Raven's thighs. Raven moaned as Johni's tongue traced her body. She didn't want to hurt Johni so she fought the urge to move into her. As if she sensed Raven's reluctance, Johni pulled her down further. Raven's body quivered and Johni moaned as she explored Raven's lower body. She worked her mouth until she started to feel Raven taking over. Raven started to move into Johni and work her body so that she was in control. Raven found it impossible to stop. She couldn't think about anything except the feeling of Johni's tongue. Johni groaned loudly as Raven worked her body faster and harder. She felt Johni's mouth open wider as Johni drank in all of her. Raven felt herself starting to peak so she slowed down. She felt Johni tense slightly in response. Raven smiled as she laid forward and touched Johni. She felt Johni shudder. Johni moaned but she began to work her tongue again. Together in perfect time they worked each other's bodies. Raven could feel herself tighten just as Johni's started to. They worked harder and faster until, in one incredible moment, they both exploded in pleasure. Raven cried out as Johni groaned loudly. They came in wave after wave of pleasure. At last, both of them spent and smelling of each other's passions, they climbed into bed and fell into each other's arms.

* * *

Raven woke up around five-thirty. The sun was still streaming through the window but she realized that they had slept for three hours. Johni was contentedly snoring next to her, making her jealous that she was still asleep. She slipped out of bed and slid her robe back on. She padded quietly to the balcony and sliding the door open, she stepped out to the most incredible view she'd ever seen. Although they had drank champagne out here earlier, it was as though she was seeing it for the first time. Johni had made certain they got a room facing the ocean and it was well worth whatever it had cost them. The sun was just starting to sink into the horizon and the sky was a wondrous mix of oranges and reds flowing into the blue green waters below.

"Isn't that something," came a voice behind her. Raven turned to find Johni standing in the doorway running her hand through her hair. Raven loved it when she did that, it made her look so intelligent and genuine. Johni, wrapped in her own robe, stepped out and joined her. She stood behind Raven sliding her arms around Raven's waist. They watched the sun as it sank lower into the ocean.

"Isn't it beautiful," Raven cooed. Johni nodded and smiled.

"The natives say that if you listen carefully you can hear the sun sizzle as it hits the water." Johni whispered. Raven looked back over her shoulder, skeptical. "Really," Johni insisted, "Listen." They both stood perfectly still and listened. As the sun lowered into the horizon Raven thought that just for a moment she might have actually heard a sound. She looked at Johni in wonder.

"Wow," she said quietly. "Now I know why you miss this place so much." Johni smiled and nodded again.

"Yeah. I had some good times here. Ricki and I both did. I understand why she would want to get married here," Johni said looking out over the water. The tides were shifting and now the waves were coming in a little harder. Raven pulled Johni's arms around her tighter.

"You weren't real sure about this wedding were you," Raven asked. Johni took a deep breath. Raven felt her tense a little. She had picked up on Johni's misgivings but they hadn't discussed it yet.

"No and I suppose I should tell you why," Johni started, "Do you remember that dinner party where we first met Whitney?"

"Yes, you were quiet about your thoughts on Whitney then too. What's up? Did she hit on you or something?" Johni smiled, can't get anything past this woman, she thought.

"As a matter of fact, she did. When I went into the kitchen for another beer she pushed up on me at the fridge," Johni explained. Raven turned around to face her and Johni could see that she was ready to pounce. Johni put a hand up. "I took care of it," she added, "but I didn't say anything because I thought that this thing Ricki had for her was just a passing fancy. I didn't realize it would come to this." Raven calmed visibly but Johni could tell that she still had her hackles up.

"That little bitch," Raven said turning back around to

face the water. She drew Johni's arms around her again. "Pushing up on my woman. Who the hell does she think she is?!" Johni smiled. She enjoyed Raven's possessiveness.

"Now baby," Johni soothed, "I took care of it. Nobody's gonna get to me. I couldn't live without you."

"You couldn't live without the sex," Raven teased.

"Well, yeah, that too," Johni added. Raven stepped firmly on her foot.

"Oh now baby, you know I love you," Johni assured her as she turned her around to face her. Johni kissed Raven lightly on the forehead, then the nose, then her lips. Raven responded once she got to her lips. After a minute Raven pushed back and walked to the edge of the balcony.

"I'll let it go this time but if she tries something like that again, she'll deal with me," she stated sternly. Johni smiled; she knew that Raven meant it. She hugged her again.

"That's my girl," Johni whispered.

"Woman!" Raven corrected. Johni laughed.

"Okay...that's my woman."

"That's better," Raven said. She kissed Johni on the cheek and went back into the room.

Chapter 6

They were supposed to meet Ricki and Whitney at six thirty but, as usual, they were late. Raven couldn't be on time to save her life. Usually when Johni wanted her there on time she had to tell her that they needed to be where ever they were going at least a half hour earlier than scheduled. But Ricki would be late too, of this Johni was sure. Ricki will be late to her own funeral as sure as the sun comes up every day. Over the years Johni had never been able to figure out why this happened; it wasn't like Ricki was the typical "girl" with the makeup, the clothes and all the other feminine trappings. It was just something that happened.

Neither Johni nor Raven realized that they were actually late too until there was a loud knock at the door; needless to say their afternoon had run away with them. Johni peered out of the bathroom at Raven who was looking up from the mirror. After a moment's hesitation they realized that it had to be Ricki at the door.

"Told you," Johni said laughing.

"Oh shut up," Raven countered lightly as she went to answer the door. Johni had warned her roughly a half hour ago that it was getting late. She had insisted to Johni that it would only be one more minute and that had been twenty-five minutes ago. She couldn't help it. She was always late, however that could be justified to a degree because with Raven she did have all the makeup and clothes and "girly" things going on. Straightening her dress, Raven opened the door to find Ricki standing with her hands on her hips. Raven put up a hand.

"I don't want to hear it. If I'm *always* late then no one should be surprised."

"She's got you there," Johni added as she came from the bathroom. Ricki smiled.

"That she does," she agreed. She patted Johni on the arm as a show of solidarity and then sat on the side of the bed as Raven finished. "At least you're here."

"Where's Whitney?" Raven asked gathering up the last of the contents that would occupy her already over stuffed purse.

"She's downstairs. She hates elevators so I came up alone," Ricki answered.

"Where are we going?" Johni asked shoving her wallet into her back pocket. Instantly Raven was behind her straightening and fixing. Johni huffed slightly and then stood still. Hell the way Raven acted sometimes you'd think that she'd never dressed herself before. Ricki smiled as she watched and Johni made a face at her.

"I thought we'd take them to The Galley."

"Good choice," Johni said as Raven stopped adjusting her. "You're going to like it Doc, it's a classy place, piano bar and all." Raven grabbed Johni's arm indicating that she was finally ready to go. She loved it when Johni called her Doc. It was a nickname Johni had given her about six months before when she'd mistakenly received some mail addressed to Dr. Raven Michaels. She had teased her by calling her Dr. Michaels for weeks but then she shortened it to Doc and now it was less annoying and instead endearing.

"It sounds wonderful. Ready to go?" Raven asked looking from Johni to Ricki as if it had been her waiting for them. Both the other women laughed; Raven just looked innocent. "What?"

"You make us late and then you ask if we are ready to go," Johni said through her laughter, "You, baby, are something else." Raven finally gave up the ghost and laughed too.

"That's what they tell me," she stated rather arrogantly. She led the way out with Ricki and Johni in tow, still laughing.

* * *

The Galley was indeed a classy place. Located in the Hilton International Hotel in Agana, the restaurant was actually on the beach. In order to get to the restaurant you had to pass through The Tree Bar which was an actual bar built around the base of a very large tree. Raven decided to talk to Johni about coming back to the bar alone when she saw some of the multicolored drinks being served and the fried scallops on the bar instead of peanuts for bar food; how cool was that?

In the restaurant itself the large floor to ceiling plate glass windows faced the ocean and the lights on the boats and harbor shone through beautifully. Ricki had managed to reserve a table at the windows which thrilled Raven. Johni held Raven's chair out for her, she smiled and sat down. The elegance with which The Galley restaurant had been put together was amazing. Each table has enough room around it that you could have dinner and conversation without having to worry about bothering anyone else. She smiled at Johni and squeezed her hand; she loved this little trip already. The main floor of the restaurant was dimly lit in order to allow for the harbor lights to appear more prominently and you could hear the ocean waves lapping the shore just outside. The tables were draped in the finest linen and the silver was meticulously polished. The restaurant was designed to hold only a certain number of guests and Raven was sure Ricki had to pull a few strings to get them reservations. There was a piano bar in the middle of the room where the piano player sat taking request from a couple who seemed to be enjoying an after dinner drink. He was an elegant looking older gentleman who smiled frequently and appeared to be enjoying his plight in life. If he didn't want to be there, it didn't show. Raven's exploration of the restaurant was interrupted by Johni, who was asking her if she wanted a drink.

"A white wine would be nice," Raven answered. For the first time she noticed the steward standing at their table. He was dressed to perfection and his clothes fit him well. He smiled as he noticed Raven's appreciation. She smiled back, nodding slightly. Drinks ordered, they all settled into conversation about the wedding.

"So do you have everything ready?" Raven asked Whitney who had arrived in an elegant white dress that seemed suited for the beach. Although she was being polite, in the back of her mind she still held a bit of an irritation that this woman had hit on Johni. She shook it off; she had promised Johni to let it go for Ricki.

"Almost," Whitney answered as the steward came back with their drinks. Raven noted that Whitney had ordered a beer like Johni and Ricki had. She had to fight to suppress the giggle welling up inside her; the woman dresses the part, Raven thought, but she doesn't act it. "You and Johni are the last of the guests to arrive."

"What else is new," Johni mused under her breath. Raven nudged her. "Just kidding." Raven smiled and took Johni's hand under the table. She had been aware of the way Whitney was looking at Johni since they first came downstairs. She might let an early discretion go but if she were to try it again, well...she would not let that go. Raven leaned into Johni slightly and kissed her on the cheek. Before the night was out Whitney would know that Johni was taken....for good.

"Where are you going to do it?" Johni asked Ricki. Raven nudged Johni harder this time. "What?" Johni asked nudging Raven back.

"They aren't "doing it", they're getting married. Why do you have to make it sound so Neanderthal?" Raven asked rolling her eyes. They all laughed.

"I didn't mean to sound Neanderthal. Whitney, my apologies. It's just that all this showiness is definitely a feminine thing," Johni answered. "Right Rick?" Ricki looked at Whitney and then back at Johni.

"Oh, I don't know," Ricki said putting an arm around Whitney, "I kind of like it."

"Oh brother," Johni said sarcastically, "Throw off the lines people this ship is lost at sea." They all laughed and Ricki leaned forward.

"Hey, try not to get me in too much trouble on this one, okay?" Johni laughed.

"Okay, I got you," Johni answered. Raven shook her head.

"You two are pathetic." They all laughed.

* * *

Dinner was wonderful. They talked about the wedding and the island. It appeared that Raven was the only person in their party who had never been here before. The other three were excited to be back. Raven sat and listened as Johni and Ricki talked about their days here in the service. It all made her wish she'd been here too. As the night wore on Raven's dislike for Whitney waned. Whitney was charming and polite and seemed to really care for Ricki. Maybe they had been wrong and maybe what had happened with Johni had just been a woman flirting; hell from time to time Raven had been accused of that herself. After dinner was over Ricki ordered a bottle of champagne and they all went down to the beach right in front of the restaurant. A number of gazebos had been erected for guests to sit and enjoy their drinks in the ocean breezes. Johni and Ricki led them to the one furthest from the restaurant. Ricki popped the cork and after each of them had a glass Ricki raised hers to make a toast.

"Here's to my friends, excuse me, our friends, joining us in what will become the happiest day of our lives. And here is to my beautiful bride," Ricki toasted. They all drank from their glasses and then kissed their mates. Raven stood with the island breeze in her hair. The smell of the ocean in the air and the sound of the waves coming in made her almost giddy. She hugged Johni tightly and enjoyed the moment. After they finished their second glass of champagne Ricki and Whitney excused themselves claiming a very early and busy next morning. Raven and Johni thanked them for dinner and watched as they made their way back to the restaurant. Once Ricki and Whitney were out of sight Johni and Raven sat down and snuggled, enjoying the beach. The night was cool and clear. There were no lights except the small ones that lit the path to the gazebos. The stars were bright and many. Raven snuggled close to Johni and gave her a kiss on the cheek.

"This is wonderful."

"Yes it is," Johni responded, kissing Raven back. "I always loved it here. I use to say if I ever settled out of the country it would be here." Raven sighed and looked up at the stars. This was perfect. The night sky, the company, everything was just perfect. Johni must have read her mind because she sighed too. They sat for a while neither of them saying a word; they enjoyed the silence together. That was something Raven could only remember doing with Walker. Walker. She really missed him sometimes. He had been her best friend after their mutual separation and when he died she was positive that she would never again share that kind of commitment with anyone else. Thank God, she had been wrong. Johni was a female version of Walker. She had his patience and his strength. If she had believed in reincarnation she would have sworn that Johni was actually Walker back from the beyond. Some of the simplest things about Johni often reminded her of him and enjoying the silence together happened to be one of those things. She often wondered why she had been chosen to be so blessed not once but twice in this life. She looked up at Johni's profile; such strength. Raven just believed that with Johni around nothing and no one could hurt her. Tears welled up in her eyes. She was happy beyond her wildest dreams. Johni looked down and seeing Raven's tears, became immediately concerned and kissed her forehead.

"I'm okay," Raven offered, "just happy." Johni smiled.

"Me too."

"Johni?"

"Yeah?"

"Can we get married here someday?" Raven asked quietly. Johni looked at her surprised. When Johni had first asked Raven to marry her she was ecstatic but then, after the trouble with Andi, she had backed off completely. She had assured Johni that she did indeed still want to get married but after the mess with Andi she needed to wait. Secretly, Johni had been crushed. Now, here she was bringing it up again, on her own.

"I thought you wanted to wait," Johni asked cautiously. Raven smiled.

"I did, but being here and seeing how happy Ricki and Whitney are, well I just wonder if we aren't overdue," Raven offered.

"You know me, just say the word," Johni said. She would marry Raven today, here, now, if she'd have her. Raven snuggled closer.

"It's a thought," Raven answered. Johni fell quiet again. Raven knew that the marriage thing was entirely up to her. Johni had made it abundantly clear that she would marry her at the drop of a hat. To some degree, Raven had felt guilty waiting but after the whole scene with her former girlfriend, Andi, marriage had become a huge step for her. Andi had seemed like a nice enough person when they had first met her. Things had gone okay during the first couple of years they were together and then, all hell broke loose. Now, after Andi had terrorized Johni and herself, Raven had to seriously re-think her instincts. She thought she knew Andi, but as it turned out she had been dead wrong...almost literally. Raven looked out over the ocean and then at Johni. Johni was different though; of this she was absolutely sure. Johni was romantic and kind and she took care of Raven. So why should she put her off like this? Still, she wasn't ready, but, she had to admit that she was more ready right now than she had been since all of this stuff with Andi had happened. She got up and walked to the edge of the gazebo. After a moment she felt Johni behind her. Johni wrapped her up in her arms and Raven felt safe.

"What are you thinking about," Johni whispered in her

ear.

"Things," Raven responded.

"Oh? Anything I can help with?"

"No," Raven answered. "It's nothing earth shattering, really."

"Oh," Johni responded nuzzling Raven's neck. Raven leaned back into Johni and felt the safe haven of her strength.

"I love you," Raven said quietly.

"I love you too Doc," Johni responded letting out a content sigh.

"Everything is just perfect here," Raven breathed.

"Yep," Johni said smiling, looking up at the stars.

"Absolutely perfect," Raven said again as she turned and slipped her arms around Johni's neck. "Nothing can touch us here, nothing at all."

Chapter 7

Johni and Raven got an early start so they could get in some sight-seeing before they finishing their preparations for the wedding. Johni was to be Ricki's best person and Raven had a list of things they would have to do to prepare for this important role. Raven would simply have no woman of hers looking half done for such an event. Johni knew that fighting her would be pointless so she just gave in and went with the flow. On the way into Agana, Guam's main village, Raven took in the sights as Johni ran down the history of the island.

"Guam was a major factor in World War I," she was explaining. "When I was here in the service, people were always finding live rounds in the jungle. The brass was always telling us that if we found anything that looked long and shiny leave it alone."

"You mean to tell me that there were still actual bombs out there?" Raven asked looking out into the underbrush. She couldn't imagine what it must feel like to look down and discover that you were standing on a live bomb.

"Yep. The Navy has to come up from the base to detonate them. They do it on the beach and it really is something to see," Johni said turning the car off the road. They had reached Agana Harbor and Johni was looking for a parking space.

"What's here?" Raven asked looking around. There were quite a few boats in the harbor waters and the wharf area was teaming with people. There were tourist, as well as fishermen, milling around and a few older looking men were seated on the pier pilings mending fishing nets. It was like something out of a painting; she was fascinated by the whole scene. Whatever Johni had in mind was fine but Raven could have just walked around and looked.

"Food," Johni answered getting out of the rental and coming around to Raven's door. She opened the door and offered her hand which Raven took.

"Is that all you think about?" Raven chided her. Johni favored with her classic give-me-a-break look. Raven smiled and squeezed Johni's hand. "Just teasing," she added. She always gave Johni a hard time about eating. Johni loved food. She didn't really over eat but she was the first person Raven had ever met that ate just for the sheer enjoyment of it. She took Raven's ribbing with a grain of salt but it remained a game they played. As she let Johni lead her to the pier she got a whiff of the air for the first time. Mixed in with the sea air were wonderful aromas of what Raven could only assume were island dishes. She'd never smelled anything like this in her life. Johni must have guessed that she had finally caught the smell in the air because she was smiling back at her.

"You were saying," Johni goaded.

"What are those heavenly scents?" Raven asked trying to follow her nose. Johni led her to an area were booths lined the walkway. People were lined up at every one of them. Raven watched as people left the lines with plates that were over flowing with food. People were laughing and having a good time. She looked at Johni who was also surveying the crowd. Johni appeared almost proud; it was funny and endearing.

"Welcome," Johni said, "to the Farmer's market. Any kind of island food you can think of is here. Everyone all over the island comes here at least once a week to eat. It's a huge tourist pull but the islanders themselves come down to eat as well. The mood is great and the people are the friendliest in the world. This was always one of my favorite spots. The guys and I would come down here sometimes two or three times a week; and it's not expensive." Raven listened to Johni and watched the crowd. It was obvious that everyone was enjoying themselves. Johni took her hand and lead her over to one of the closest booths. They started there and hit four more before they finally went looking for a place to sit. Raven couldn't believe all the food they had on their plates. Johni got her settled and went to fetch their drinks. When she returned, Raven had already eaten her way through a forth of her plate. She couldn't believe how wonderful the food was. Johni sat down across from her laughing.

"Didn't I tell you that it would be good," she asked opening a Pepsi for Raven. She just shook her head and kept on eating. Johni opened her own soda and dug in herself. By the time Raven bothered to speak again over half her plate was empty.

"This is really good," she said draining the last of her soda.

"I told you," Johni said chewing on a rib. "I really love the island food. It's some of the best in the world, in my opinion." Raven nodded her agreement. She sat back for a moment to take a breath. She was really stuffed but she still wanted to finish the food on her plate. Johni pushed her plate forward.

"I don't think I can eat another bite," she said. Raven pushed her plate forward as well.

"I'll get a take-out box," Johni offered, getting up. Raven watched her as she went back to the nearest booth. She loved to watch her walk. She had such a masculine way about her and she really took special care of her; she did everything in her power to make Raven comfortable. Sometimes she felt guilty because as hard as Johni tried, she still found herself complaining at times; it wasn't right and Raven knew it but she just couldn't help it; it was in her blood. Hell, she was just spoiled. Johni came back with the container and stopped just shy of the table. She stood looking at Raven which made her smile.

"What?" Raven asked innocently. Johni smiled and shook her head.

"You're up to something. I can tell by the look on your face."

"Me?" Raven feigned surprise. Johni laughed as she reached for the plates to put the food into the box she'd just gotten. Raven reached out and put a hand on Johni's.

"Why don't you let me do that," she said taking the box from Johni. Johni gladly let it go and sat down as Raven finished putting their food away. She watched her with an admiration that tickled her every time she caught her doing it. She often did it when she thought Raven wasn't watching. One thing was for sure she would never let her forget the extent of her love for her; it was one of Johni's most endearing qualities. Neither of them were ever at a loss for words when it came to telling the other how they felt but Johni was especially open about her feelings. They had been through some harrowing times together when neither of them were sure if they'd be around to enjoy their love so it made their time together now even more special. After almost losing Johni to a car accident and then cancer, Raven was thankful for every moment they spent together. Johni winked at her and went to put the food in the car. Raven watched her go. Life hadn't been easy on Johni although it didn't show. Over the last year Raven had found out enough about Johni's life to realize that she'd carried around a lot of pain for many years. Johni's mother had tried to abort her before she was born. Unaware that she had been carrying twins, her mother had in actuality only aborted one fetus and Johni had survived three months premature; despite her mother's best efforts, she'd made it into the world anyways. Johni's mother had managed to carry her anger towards the baby she hadn't wanted throughout Johni's childhood. She had thwarted Johni's every effort to have a "normal" life. She fulfilled Johni's basic needs for shelter and clothing but the love just wasn't there. Johni's emotional well-being seemed to escape the concern of her mother. To make matters worse when Johni turned six her father started molesting her. The abuse lasted six years before Johni had finally found the voice to say anything. She had run away from home to a friend's home and her friend's mother had called the local police in an effort to help. In a time when child abuse was not such a hot button topic Johni was branded a trouble maker and released back into the care of an uncaring mother and an abusive father. Johni had said that although her father had not touched her again after her revelation, his loathing and contempt for her was apparent always. She was always the outsider.

Johni ended up raising herself with the help of a caring grandmother who did her best to make up for all of the pain her own daughter was causing her grandchild. Raven had to admit that she had done a good job too. Johni appeared to be a very well-adjusted person despite all of the pain. One had to be very close to her in order to understand the pain she carried with her; she didn't trust many people. Raven did everything she could to ease the pain of Johni's past but it was difficult for her at times. Raven herself had been sheltered all her life. Her family and friends had always protected her from the world and all its evils. Hell, Raven grew up in a household with brothers and she couldn't even imagine any of them attempting to look at her cross-eyed let alone touching her inappropriately. In the meantime she did everything she could to help Johni through the bad times. One thing was for sure, as far as she was concerned, as long as there was a breath in her, she would make sure that Johni would never again feel alone. She loved her with all her heart and no one would ever hurt her again. Lost in thought she hadn't even noticed Johni standing on the other side of the table again. Johni cleared her throat and Raven looked up.

"Penny for your thoughts," Johni said smiling. Raven looked appalled.

"Excuse me? A penny? I don't know who you think you're talking to but a penny wouldn't even cover the first letter of the first sentence of my thoughts."

"Oh?" Johni asked with one eyebrow raised. "A little arrogant aren't we?" Raven smiled a sly little smile and got up from the table. She joined Johni on the other side and grabbed her arm.

"I know what I know," she stated simply. Johni laughed.

"You're rotten."

"Thank you," Raven answered. "What next?" She was eager to get on with their day. She knew that whatever Johni had planned she would enjoy it.

"Well how about a hike up the beach," Johni offered. She pointed towards the sand and the cliffs.

"Okay," Raven answered heading in the direction Johni was pointing. Johni laughed and caught up to her.

"Hey, can I go too," she asked. Raven favored her with a side glance and walked a little faster.

"Okay, but keep up." They both laughed as they headed for the first set of dunes.

Chapter 8

The coastline of Guam was incredible. Johni and Raven had walked for some time before the stopped and sat down in the sand to rest. Walking in sand is not small chore so they both needed the stop. Raven knew that Johni would be having slight problems with her right knee. Several years ago she'd had it replaced and now and then it gave her problems. As she suspected when they sat down Johni was rubbing the knee and grimacing slightly.

"Are you okay?" Raven asked. Johni smiled at her and nodded.

"I only ache a little."

"I don't know why you insist on doing things like this when it's only going to hurt." Raven said in a frustrated voice. She stayed on Johni about taking care of herself. Not that Johni really listened, although at times she pretended to.

"I can't stop living just because of a little pain." Johni answered pulling Raven's arm so that she'd move closer to her. "Besides I have to keep up with you." Raven feigned surprise.

"Me?"

"Yes you." Johni said laughing. "Don't pretend not to know that you are the healthiest forty-three year old woman on the planet." Raven laughed with her. She had to admit she was pretty healthy for her age. She enjoyed life and it showed. She snuggled a little closer to Johni as they watched the waves roll in. It was so peaceful here. There was no one else on the beach but them.

"Where are we headed?" Raven asked. She hadn't asked but now she was just a little curious. They had been walking a ways.

"Up the beach a bit farther." Johni answered indicating the direction with her head. "There's a cliff called Lover's Leap and we will be at the base of it. I use to snorkel there sometimes. It's beautiful." Raven smiled and squeezed Johni's arm.

"It sounds nice. Why do they call it Lover's Leap?"

"Along time ago there was this island princess and she fell in love with a boy from another village." Johni explained. "Her father had forbidden her to marry outside her own village but the princess continued to meet with the boy secretly until a spiteful girl from the boys village told the princess's father what was happening. The boy was brought to the Chief and when he refused to stop seeing the princess the Chief sentenced him to die. The warriors from the princess's village took the boy up to the cliffs and threw him off while the princess watched. Over wrought with despair the princess then ran past her father and right in front of him and the people of her village threw herself off the cliff after her lover. Ever since, it's been known as

Lover's Leap. You'd be amazed at how many couples have followed suit since then."

"You mean other couples have actually thrown themselves off the cliffs?" Raven asked appalled.

"Yep." Johni confirmed. "When Ricki and I were here in the service an Airman First Class and his wife did it; seems they'd just discovered that she was going to die of some disease." Raven shook her head.

"I love you but," she started but Johni stopped her.

"I know me too. Seems a bit extreme. The airman was from our squadron but Ricki refused to go to the funeral. She said it was a stupid way to die."

"Did you go?" Raven asked already knowing the answer. Johni was an extremely compassionate person.

"Yep. It was the least I could do. Besides I was shop chief, I kind of had to." Johni answered thoughtfully.

"You would have gone anyway." Raven stated. Johni smiled. She knew Raven was right.

"Well you ready to head out?" Johni asked getting up and brushing the sand off.

"Let's go." Raven said putting her hand out so that Johni could help her up. Johni pulled her right up, almost off her feet. Raven laughed and hugged her around the neck.

"You are so strong." She whispered in her ear. Johni blushed slightly, which was why Raven said things like that to her.

"Come on." Johni said pulling Raven towards the direction they were to continue. Raven laughed and let herself be pulled.

* * *

They walked for another half hour before they reached the last outcropping before Lover's Leap. Raven had noticed that the water did indeed seem to be bluer her then it had been down the beach. She mentioned this to Johni.

"It's beautiful isn't it?" Johni said looking out over the water proudly. Raven had to smile. You'd think it was her own personal island, Raven thought. Johni caught her smile.

"What?"

"Nothing." Raven answered. "Just admiring you. You're going to look really good in a tux."

"You think so?" Johni asked. "I wish I'd dropped about ten pounds."

"You're going to look fine. Ricki will be proud to have you at her sie." Raven answered. Johni smiled.

"I'm going to be proud to be there for her. Who would have guessed that she'd get married first?" Johni added.

"You two have been friends for a while huh?" Raven asked. She envied Johni and Ricki's friendship. She herself had never had many close friends. Having close friends meant having to maintain them and she just didn't have time. She realized that it sounded harsh but she really didn't. When you had friends you had to keep in touch and all that. She just wasn't good at that.

"We've been through a lot." Johni confirmed. "She had gotten on my nerves but all in all she's been a good friend. One of my best." They rounded the last outcropping and the first thing both of them noticed was a small crowd of people at the base of the next cliff.

"That's strange," Johni said, a bewildered look on her face. "There aren't usually many people out here. Raven looked up and noticed that there were people looking over the edge of the cliffs above as well. She pointed this out to Johni.

"What do you think they are all interested in?" Raven asked heading to the crowd. Johni hesitated and then followed her. She had an idea but didn't want to believe it. As they approached the crowd they both picked up words here and there. By the time they reached the crowd Johni's worse fear was confirmed. Someone had jumped. How bizarre, she thought, that she would be telling Raven the story only to come up here and find and example. She reached out and grabbed Raven's arm.

"Doc, you don't want to go up there." Johni said looking up ahead to a smaller crowd gathered in the rocks.

"Someone jumped." Raven whispered astounded.

"It looks like it." Johni confirmed. She started back the way they'd come when she realized that Raven wasn't in tow. "Raven...." She started but Raven was already heading for the rocks. Damn, Johni thought and then followed her. Raven had a morbid fascination with things of this nature. She always had this battle with herself about whether or not she really wanted to see only to lose to her own curiosity. Later, when she had nightmares she'd wish she hadn't come up. As they reached the place where the smaller crowd had gathered Raven noted that there were ropes coming down the face of the cliff. A carrier, like those the coast guard used, was leaning up against the face of the cliff. They must have to bring the body out that way, Raven surmised. For the first time she saw several people in uniform. They were trying to shoo the crowd away but the onlookers weren't having it. Raven edged her way up to the place in the rocks that had everyone so interested. She felt Johni right behind her. She knew she shouldn't be up here. She knew she shouldn't look but something compelled her to do it anyway. They reached a point where they could see the body and Raven braced herself and looked over into the small crevice in which the body lay. She gasped and threw her hand over her mouth to keep from screaming. She heard Johni behind her and knew that she should turn around but she couldn't. Some uncontrollable force held her there. She heard Johni let out a small cry and suddenly she was in front of Raven gazing down at the twisted mangled body. There in the crevice before them staring up, with unseeing eyes, was Ricki

Chapter 9

Raven brought Johni a cup of tea and sat down opposite her on the terrace. Although the climate was tropical, Raven felt chilled. She reached over and laid a hand on Johni's knee. Johni's only response was to look up. She had been quite shaken by the sight of Ricki at the base of Lover's Leap. Raven had to drag her away from the scene after they'd spoken to Paul Greyson, the police detective in charge. When Greyson noticed Johni and Raven's reaction he came over and asked if they'd known the victim. The word victim caught their attention. After they told him who they were, Greyson walked them away from the crowd and explained that whether it be suicide, murder or an accident, Ricki was still considered a victim. They explained to Greyson who she was and why they were in Guam. Raven did most of the talking. Johni kept looking back in the direction of the body and Raven surmised that she must be in shock. After she explained everything she knew, the police detective asked about Whitney. This instantly snapped Johni out of her stupor. She questioned Greyson on what he knew. All he could offer was that two divers had happened upon the body. Johni insisted on having a look around after that. The detective allowed it as long as she didn't touch anything. They stayed until the body had been removed and Raven had to convince Johni that they should leave. Johni hardly said a word during the walk and the drive back to the hotel. She opened the hotel room door and headed straight for the phone. She dialed Ricki's room and got no answer. Raven ordered some tea and insisted that Johni go sit down. As she looked up at her Raven realized just how close Ricki and Johni had been. The look on Johni's face made her heart ached for something to say but, truth be told, she hardly knew Ricki. She'd met her through Johni and although they had spent time together, she still couldn't say they'd gotten very close. She did, however, enjoy Ricki's company and was sad to lose a friend. Johni, however, was hurting deeply. She and Ricki had spent time together for the last ten years or so. Johni got up and walked to the balcony railing. Gazing out across the ocean she took a deep breath and spoke quietly. Raven joined her so that she could hear everything she was saying.

"I just don't understand, Doc," Johni started. "She would never do something like that to herself so who would want to hurt her?" Raven took a deep breath. This was always the hard part of their relationship. Johni needed to ask questions and it was Raven who would play the devil's advocate. It was an uncomfortable position but Raven knew Johni well enough to know that it was what she needed.

"How do you know she wouldn't have done it?"

"She was afraid of heights," Johni snapped. "She hated even being up there. She said it gave her the creeps." Johni took a breath to calm down. In her mind she knew what Raven was doing but her emotions were having another reaction entirely. She softened a bit. "Why would you ask such a question?"

"People do some crazy things," Raven offered. "Anything could have provoked her. Maybe Whitney left her or told her something she didn't want to live with. We don't know the whole story." Johni put her head down and rubbed her eyes.

"Whitney," She spat out. "Like to know where the hell she is." Raven shared her sentiments there. Where was Whitney? Was she somehow involved? Raven turned to sit back down when there was a knock at the door. She looked back at Johni who then stepped passed her to answer it. Raven followed closely. Johni looked through the peep hole in the door and then pulled it open. Paul Greyson, the detective from the beach, and a man they didn't recognized stood at the door.

"Hello," Greyson said extending a hand to Johni. "I was hoping we could talk to you." Johni shook the detectives offered hand and then stepped back to let the two men enter.

"Sure, come on in." They stepped inside and Johni closed the door.

"Come this way," Raven said leading the way, "we can talk out on the terrace." After they were all seated Greyson cleared his throat.

"This is my partner, Sam Rhodes," He said indicating the other man. "We came over to ask you about Whitney Rodgers." Johni and Raven glanced at each other.

"What about her?" Johni asked taking the lead. Raven almost smiled. She liked it when she took charge.

"How well did you know her?" Greyson asked. Johni took a minute before she answered. She didn't want her own suspicions about Whitney to over shadow the way she answered.

"Not real well," Johni answered cautiously. "She was engaged to Ricki but we really didn't get to know her that well. She wasn't very personable at first but Ricki loved her and frankly, if Ricki cared about her, she was okay with me." Raven nodded her agreement.

"Did Ricki ever discuss Whitney's past with you at all?" Detective Rhodes asked. It was the first time he'd chosen to speak. His voice was a very low bass and it made Raven think of Barry White. He wasn't a tall man. Judging from his skin tone and features he was probably an island native. He looked intriguing. Not handsome, not ugly but somewhere in-between.

"Not really," Johni was answering. "Ricki was, well, sort of just taken with Whitney. They hadn't know each other very long. In fact, we were surprised when she announced that they were getting married."

"How long had they known each other?" Greyson asked leaning slightly forward in his seat.

"About two months," Johni answered and the detectives glanced at each other. Raven watched them both trying to figure out what was going on. As if she read her mind, Johni asked the question that was obviously on both their minds.

"What's going on Detective?" Greyson cleared his throat.

"Did Ricki have any enemies?" He asked sternly. Johni laughed incredulously.

"Enemies? Ricki? You have got to be kidding. Hell no, she didn't have any enemies."

"What about Whitney?" Rhodes asked.

"I told you," Johni answered, "we really didn't know Whitney all that well. We would have no idea who her friends were let alone her enemies."

"When was the last time you saw Ricki alive?" Greyson prodded. Johni was

"I guess last night," She answered quietly. "We all went to dinner at The Galley."

"And Whitney? When was the last time you saw her?" Greyson added. The questions were getting tedious now. Raven felt it and she could see it on Johni's face.

"Last night," Raven answered this time. "Detective what is going on? Did Whitney have anything to do with Ricki's death?" Johni reached over and took Raven's hand. She was obviously grateful having the question out in the open. The two detectives looked at each other and then back at the two of them. Their faces were grim.

"We found Whitney Rodgers this morning, dead, a little ways down the beach from Ricki," Greyson reported. "We think she must have gone over the cliff at the same time Ricki did but she hit the water instead of the rocks." Johni squeezed Raven's hand. "We don't believe they jumped. Evidence indicates that they were pushed from the cliffs." Greyson stopped long enough for what he was saying to sink in. After a few moments he continued. "There's more. As you probably know Guam, like Hawaii, is preparing to legalize gay and lesbian marriages. The decision to do so came down last January. Since then we have had several deaths just like these. All the victims were Lesbians. All were planning to get married." Johni and Raven glanced at one another. "Obviously, we believe there is a connection between the other deaths and these. This is the first time we've had hard evidence that the deaths are murders and not suicides. It's the best break we've had so far."

"So you think someone is killing lesbians who are coming to the island to get married?" Raven asked. She was more than a little curious.

"Not all who come but enough to stir up a little bad publicity maybe. When these "suicides" hit the paper there is public outcry that legalizing the marriages is the wrong thing to do. Some islanders already believe that lesbianism is an abomination. How better to prove that than to show that they are more likely to kill themselves too. The island is mostly Catholic and Catholics believe that suicide is an unforgivable sin." Johni sat forward.

"You mean our friends might have been killed so some homophobic psychopath could prove a point?" Johni's voice conveyed her disgust and anger. Raven put a soothing hand on her shoulder, but her face mirrored Johni's sentiments.

"It appears so," Greyson answered. Johni got up and went to the railing. Raven knew that she was trying to get a handle on her anger.

"So what now?" Raven asked. Greyson again glanced at his partner. She knew that something was up. She could feel it.

"We'd like your help," Greyson said evenly.

"Excuse me," Johni said from behind Raven. Greyson cleared his throat again. Raven guessed that it must be a habit with him. As if to confirm her suspicion, he did it again.

"There's killer on the island and so far he or she has eluded us," Greyson explained. "Obviously we are seriously missing something and it is costing more and more people their lives. Maybe if we had the help of someone who knew this.......” Greyson hesitated. Raven could see in his face that he was searching for the right words. He cleared his throat yet again and then continued. “...well, this side of the street, if you will. We need the help of someone who knows the community.”

“What you need is bait,” Johni retorted in disgust. Greyson looked at Raven, pleading silently. Raven swung around to face Johni. She could see right away that there would be no discussing this with her right now. Turning back to the detectives she stood up.

“We’ll think about it,” She stated simply. The two men followed her lead and stood as well. They started towards the door. Johni hung back but Raven followed them to the door.

“We appreciate that,” Greyson said, reaching for the door. He stopped briefly to hand Raven his card. “Call us when you’ve made a decision.” Raven took his card, nodded her agreement and shut the door behind them. She turned back to the balcony. Johni stood rigidly gazing out over the ocean. Raven could hear the wind picking up slightly and the sound of the seas below collecting themselves so that they could pound the cliffs. A storm was coming, she could smell it. Again she looked to Johni. Could she convince her to help the island police to catch a killer? Could she convince Johni that it was best that they help catch the person who killed her best friend? She'd have to try. She just couldn't see leaving the island while a killer walked free, a killer they could help capture.

Chapter 10

"You actually want to go along with this?" Johni repeated for the fourth time. Raven sighed and put her head down. They had come downstairs to get something to eat in the hotel restaurant and discuss the detective's proposition. So far she'd gotten nowhere with Johni. Picking up her fork, Raven stabbed a piece of chicken and stuffed it into her mouth out of frustration. This action was not lost on Johni who smiled slowly and finally laughed out loud.

"You are so dramatic when you're pissed, you know that?" Raven tried to be angry but instead joined in the laughter.

"I am not." She half-heartedly protested. Johni favored her with a "yeah right" look and picked up her own fork.

"Why is this so important to you?" Johni asked as she played with the food on her plate. Raven had noticed that she wasn't eating much and decided not to push the issue. She realized that Ricki's death had been a big shock for Johni. She would give her a day or so before bugging her about eating.

"If we have a chance to help find Ricki's killer, shouldn't we?" Raven offered.

"It's dangerous and I don't want to put you in that kind of a situation."

"We," Raven corrected. "We would be doing it and I'm not exactly helpless you know." She hated it when Johni insisted on treating her like the weak female. Johni sighed and gave Raven a tired look.

"Why don't we let it go for tonight and sleep on it." Johni said picking up her glass of wine and draining it. Raven started to say something but noticed the look in Johni's eyes and stopped short.

She didn't want to push too hard. If she wasn't careful, Johni would say no and that would be that. Johni could be quite stubborn at times.

"Okay. What do you want to do this evening?" Raven asked, trying to change the subject. Johni looked absently out the window, obviously lost in thought.

"I don't know. We would have been making last minute preparations for the wedding," She answered quietly. The pain in her words was obvious. Raven reached over and took her hand. When Johni looked up at her there were tears in her eyes. Raven's heart ached for her.

"Why don't we go back to the room," Raven offered giving her hand a squeeze. "We could watch TV or something." Johni smiled and look relieved. They stood up and Johni put some money on the table for a tip. When they turned to go, they noticed a small crowd of people coming in. They stopped and watched as the party was seated. Raven glanced at Johni to see if she was thinking the same thing. It was obvious by the look on her face that she was. The focus of the small crowd was two women; they looked happy, anyone could see that they were a couple.

"I'll bet they're here to get married," Johni whispered, "Want to make a bet?"

"I think that's a bet I'll lose," Raven answered. They watched the couple a moment longer and then made for the door. As they were going out the door Raven stole one more glance back. They looked so happy. They looked just like Ricki and Whitney had the night before they'd died. She looked up to see Johni looking back at her. Johni reached back and took Raven's hand as if she had read her mind.

"I know", she said squeezing her hand once before heading for the room, "I know."

* * *

Raven reached for Johni and got a hand full of empty sheets. Raising her head she looked at the illuminated clock on the TV. It read 2:17 A.M. They had come back from the restaurant and crawled into bed to watch television. It hadn't taken long for either of them to fall asleep. Raven got out of bed and grabbed her role pulling it tightly around her. As her eyes adjusted to the dark she felt a breeze coming from the balcony. The sliding door stood open and the curtains were blowing in the wind.

Moving quietly but quickly she stepped to the window. Sure enough Johni was sitting on the balcony looking out over the ocean. She seemed deep in thought, so deep that she didn't notice Raven coming up behind her. She tensed slightly when Raven put her hands on her shoulders.

"Hey," Johni said putting her hands on Raven's.

"Hi, couldn't you sleep?" Raven asked slipping her arms around Johni's shoulders.

"No, I didn't want to wake you so I came out here."

"Are you okay?" Raven asked coming around to sit on the arm of Johni's chair. As she was about to sit, however, Johni pulled her around so that she sat on her lap. She snuggled up in Johni's arms as Johni hugged her.

"I'm okay," Johni said finally loosening her arms a little. "Just a lot on my mind."

"Anything I can help you with?"

"No," Johni answered kissing Raven's arm. "Got to work this out for myself." Raven snuggled in again and hugged Johni tightly. The sea air smelled of salt and the breezes blew by them as they sat on the balcony holding each other. Johni rose up and with one hand moved Raven's face close to hers. She kissed Raven first softly and then again with more urgency. Raven responded by letting herself become absorbed in Johni's embrace. Wordlessly they got up from the chair and moved into the room. They left the window open and the ocean breezes filled the room as they reached the bed touching each other. Raven could feel Johni's hunger for her and it served to excite her. She let Johni undress her, peeling away first her robe and then the gown beneath. She stood as Johni sat on the side of the bed and then allowed herself to be pulled forward. She threw her head back as Johni devoured her breasts with kisses stopping on each nipple in order to give them special attention. She groaned softly as Johni moved down her body kissing her stomach and then back up to her breast. She grabbed Johni's hair and pulled her head back so that she could fill her mouth with her tongue. Johni fell back and Raven followed crawling on top of her and straddling Johni's body. She positioned herself so that their bodies were aligned and she could feel Johni's full body on hers. She heard Johni moan as she kissed her breasts and shoulders. She might not be able to help what was on Johni's mind but she could certainly take her mind off it for a while. She moved up Johni's body and attacked her neck. Johni squirmed and laughed softly.

"You know that drives me crazy," Johni whispered.

"So lose your mind for a while," Raven whispered as she went back to nibbling on her neck. Johni moaned louder and tried to force Raven into a less aggressive position. Raven wasn't having it; she gently pushed Johni back down and smiled.

"No dice. Tonight you are going to relax and let me take care of you first."

"Oh, my very own cave woman," Johni said smiling and laying back.

"That's right," Raven said kissing Johni deeply. She let her tongue dart in and out of Johni's lips. Johni groaned as she tried to catch her tongue. Raven laughed mischievously and moved her tongue to Johni's breasts. She wrote her name with her tongue on Johni's stomach before moving between her legs. As a rule she didn't perform oral sex but now and then she liked to catch Johni off guard by making love her in this way. Although Johni was okay with the fact that oral sex was not one of Raven's methods of choice, it drove Johni crazy. Johni, startled, sat up but Raven pushed her down again. Surrendering, Johni lay back. Raven went to work using her tongue to trace Johni's pearl. It instantly came to life and Raven took a moment to smile. She latched on to Johni with her mouth and worked her tongue until Johni cried out. She came explosively and Raven had to hold onto her in order to bring her to a full orgasm. Obviously spent, Johni reached for Raven. Raven crawled up the length of Johni's body and kissed her full on the mouth. She knew that the taste of Johni's sex on her mouth was a turn on for Johni. Raven wasn't disappointed, Johni instantly came to life rolling over and handling Raven. She went about the business of gorging herself on Raven's body. She moved readily to the softness between Raven's legs and went instantly to the core of Raven with her tongue. She toyed with Raven until she was almost ready to release and stopped. Raven, appalled that Johni would stop now, looked up. Johni smiled and effortlessly turned her over on her stomach. She inserted two fingers into Raven and reached for her very essence. Raven moaned loudly as Johni worked her fingers in and out of her wetness. It didn't take long before Raven heard herself begging for the strokes to be harder and faster. Johni was more than willing to accommodate her as she moved with Raven's frantic rhythm until Raven cried out over and over again. Raven felt herself climax in wave after wave. For a moment she had the fleeting thought that she might never stop. After a few moments the waves subsided and Raven reached for Johni. They lay in each other's arms breathless.

"I love you Raven," Johni said in the dark.

"I love you too," Raven whispered snuggling closer. She lay listening to Johni's breathing until it evened out. Absently, as she started to fall asleep, she realized that the door to the balcony was still open but she didn't have the strength to get up and shut it. The sound of the waves only added to her feeling of contentment. Smiling, Raven followed Johni into sleep.

Chapter 11

"Okay."

"Really?"

"I said okay, didn't I?" Johni asked as she turned the shower on. "If you push it I might change my mind." She'd been up since four a.m. trying to decide whether it was worth it to try to catch Ricki's killer. She finally settled on, someone has to do it. She didn't particularly care for the fact that Raven would be involved. But at least they'd do it together. Ricki had been like a sister to Johni so it was important to help find her killer.

"What changed your mind?" Raven asked trying to sound casual and not nosy.

"If you keep pushing, you're libel to change it back," She answered stepping into the shower.

"Okay, okay," Raven yelled from the bedroom. Johni let the hot water stream over her. She wished the memories of seeing Ricki's body would wash away with the suds. She knew, however, that for the rest of her life this would be the last memory she'd have of her friend. What a way to die. She could just imagine Ricki's terror. She'd been afraid of heights. To die facing your worse fear had to be horrifying. Angrily Johni soaped her body. Who would do something like this? What kind of sick mind gets off on taking someone's life? If what Greyson had said was true, then whoever did this had been in business for some time. Was it a game? She meant to find out. When she discovered who was responsible, she'd make sure they paid. She'd make sure for Ricki and of course for Whitney. She turned off the water and stood for a moment to let it drain off her body, hoping it would take with it the anger she was feeling. She heard Raven come into the bathroom but purposely didn't say anything. She waited for Raven to speak first. Raven cleared her throat after a long moment of silence.

"Johni?" She asked carefully, "Are you angry with me?" Johni smiled. After all this time Raven still didn't realize that Johni didn't get angry at her, frustrated sometimes but never angry. She slid the shower door open. Raven was leaning against the counter looking concerned.

"No," Johni reassured her. "You know I can't get angry with you. You bug the hell out of me at times but you never make me angry." Raven smiled.

"Really," she fished. Johni grinned and got out of the shower. She made like she was reaching for a towel but instead grabbed Raven. "Johni!"

"What's the matter Doc?" She asked rubbing her wetness all over Raven. Raven pushed her back laughing.

"That was not right!" Raven complained trying to wipe off the water.

"What?" Johni asked innocently. Raven picked up the

towel and threw it in Johni's face.

"I'll get you back for that," She stated and left Johni to dry off. Johni finished and put her clothes on.

"I guess we should grab some breakfast and then head for the police station," Johni offered putting her keys in her pocket. Raven sat on the bed watching her. She had a sly smile on her face and Johni instantly knew what she was going to say but beat her to the punch. "I know, I know, I'm anal. I can't help that I need routine or I'll be lost." Raven laughed. Every morning Johni found herself going through a ritual. She'd shower, get dressed and then fill her pockets with certain items she usually kept with her during the day. Raven teased her about it because she would take such great care to do so even if she were not planning to leave the house. She couldn't help it if she wanted to be prepared, she'd always tell Raven.

"Do you want breakfast or not?" She asked trying to sound annoyed. Raven slid off the bed and put her arms around Johni's neck.

"Now you just said you never get angry with me so I know that sound in your voice is an act." She kissed Johni on the neck and then looked up at her smiling. "Isn't that right?" She cooed. Johni found herself responding. You're whipped Andrews, she thought as she kissed Raven back, totally whipped.

"Are you ready?" She asked, pushing Raven away half-heartedly. Raven laughed.

"Yeah, let's go." They left the room in search of food.

* * *

"If we're going to get involved in this we have to know everything." Johni was saying. They had eaten breakfast and gone straight to the island police department. Raven couldn't help but scan the room while Johni explained their wishes to the Detective. They had decided, over breakfast, to tell the police they'd help but only if they were told what they were up against. Johni and Raven both had some concerns over the police not wanting to let go of information on the case. The Detective's office was a mess. Greyson is obviously single, Raven thought looking around. He kept his office like a bachelor. It never failed to amaze her how disarrayed a person could get when they lived alone. She had never had the opportunity to find out if she would be that way. Amazingly she had never lived alone. The Island Police department was by no means small. This surprised her. She really hadn't known what to expect but she had this left over picture in her mind of grass huts for some reason. As it turned out, the department looked like any other police department she'd been in. In fact there wasn't a lot of difference between this place and the one in Seattle. Something Johni was saying dragged her attention back to the conversation at hand.

"I will not put Raven in danger," Johni was saying. "You have to let us in on it all if you want our help and that's all there is to it." Detective Greyson looked a little pale. Rhodes was too busy checking Raven out. She wasn't sure if he'd heard any of what Johni had said. She moved a little closer to Johni and put her hand on her arm. Rhodes finally took his eyes off Raven and turned to Greyson.

"She's right Paul. If you had asked me the same thing I would want to know everything too, especially in this case." Greyson considered for a moment and then nodded.

"I guess that's fair. We have four years' worth of files that you're welcome to and Sam and I will answer anything you need to know." He turned and pulled a stack of thick files from the cabinet behind him and placed them on the desk. "These are full of every bit of evidence we have on this case. I guess I don't have to ask that you not discuss it with anyone," he added. Johni nodded as Raven reached for the first file.

"I thought you said the deaths had been occurring since last January?" Raven asked as she leafed through the file. She'd have to read it later.

"I did and that's true but there were several deaths that might be connected that go back as far as four years, the first occurring in the Spring of 1993," Greyson answered.

"Connected how?" Johni asked looking over Raven's shoulder at the file in her lap.

"Well, the island has had a gay and lesbian community as long as anyone can remember. Most of the island natives who are homosexual live in Agat on the east side of the island. But before 1993 this was not a subject many people discussed. Then, in 1993, there was a huge fire at a club on Yigo beach that the gays and lesbians on the island frequented. Seventeen people were killed in that fire and all were homosexual. It was later discovered that the fire had been deliberately set and the exits had been blocked to keep people from escaping. It was really bad."

"That's awful," Raven said closing the file. "Did they catch whoever did it?"

"No," Greyson answered dropping his head. "I was in charge of the case and it was my first major loss. There just wasn't enough evidence. Whoever set that fire knew exactly what they were doing and cleaned up after themselves. A lot of things were said to strain relations between the local gay population and the community at large because those who died in the fire were living an alternative lifestyle. There were a few protests when we didn't find the killer, or killers because the gay and lesbian community felt that more could have been done."

"Was enough being done?" Raven questioned. Greyson looked pained.

"I feel there was. I worked my guys overtime on that case," He defended. "There just wasn't enough to go on."

"Anyway," Rhodes interrupted, "a few weeks after the fire a gay couple was found at the bottom of the Leap. It was ruled a suicide although there were rumors that they were murdered. The case was not widely publicized but the local newspaper, The Island Flyer, published an article about homosexuals being prone to suicide."

"That's ridiculous," Raven said. She felt Johni's hand on her shoulder. It was Johni's way of telling her not to get started. She tried to calm down.

"I agree," Rhodes said. "But it started people to talking and one thing led to another and suddenly there was a group organized to protect gay rights and another organized to take those rights away. The two have been fighting ever since. Last January the Hawaiian government was presented with a bill to legalize gay and lesbian marriages. The local government realized how much it was going to do for the Hawaiian economy and decided to beat them to it. Since the bill was made public a year and a half ago, seven couples have met the same fate. Your friends make it eight. Needless to say something is drastically wrong here." Johni stood up.

"Can we take these back to our hotel?"

"I don't see why not," Greyson said standing as well.

"Does that mean you'll help?" Raven looked at Johni.

"We'll see," Johni answered. Raven stood as Johni collected the files. "Why don't you plan to come by tomorrow morning so we can discuss it further?"

"Okay, I'm hoping you can help us, Ms. Andrews," Greyson said walking them to the door. "I would really like to catch whoever is responsible for this."

"We'll talk to you tomorrow," Johni said. They left the station and neither of them said a word until they were almost half way back to the hotel. Raven finally broke the silence.

"I believe him," she offered.

"About what?"

"That he wants to catch whomever is responsible."

"I do too," Johni agreed. "You really want to do this don't you?"

"I do," Raven said looking out the window, "Don't you?" Johni appeared to be thoughtful for a moment.

"I guess I do, I'm just leery of getting you involved in something where you might get hurt."

"Johni, I'm not helpless."

"I know, but I feel responsible for you and I will protect you at all costs," Johni stated strongly. Raven got a warm feeling inside. Johni wanted to protect her and it felt wonderful. She slid closer and put her arm in Johni's.

"I think that's great but this needs to be done and I promise to be careful." Johni looked skeptical.

"Do you know how?" She asked turning into the hotel parking lot. Raven slapped her arm and slid back over to her side of the car.

"Yes, I do," she answered grudgingly. Johni reached out and squeezed her hand.

"I love you and it would kill me if anything happened to you. Let's face it Doc, you're not exactly watchful." Raven folded her arms but said nothing. Johni was right and she knew it.

"You'll be there to protect me," she offered. Johni smiled and kissed Raven on the nose. Normally she liked this show of affection but right now she felt like Johni was using it in the way that a man would dismiss some silly idea from his wife. She frowned and pushed away from Johni.

"I'm a lot more self-sufficient than you're giving me credit for," she protested. Johni sat back and favored her with a smile.

"I know, Doc. Just do me a favor. If we decide to do this thing, let's do it together. Okay?" Raven squirmed at the implication that she would do otherwise but then gave in.

"Okay, I promise."

"Good," Johni said, apparently satisfied with her answer. "Feel like a little light reading?" She added grabbing up the thick files between them.

"A little," Raven answered getting out of the car.

"Well then, let's order room service and get to it," Johni said laughing. She fell into step with Raven and they headed for their room.

Chapter 12

"Can you believe this?" Raven asked dropping the last file onto the already overwhelming stack. Johni didn't offer an answer but instead just shook her head. They had spent the better part of the day reading through the stack of files Greyson had given them. Each file was a different case but after reading through them all only an idiot wouldn't see a connection. Sixteen people, eight couples, in eighteen months. That was two shy of a body a month. All the couples fell to their deaths. Not all were necessarily at the Leap but those that weren't actually at the Leap were nearby.

"You want a drink?" Johni asked reaching for the phone.

"Yes, a wine spritzer." Raven watched as Johni called room service. She was concerned about how hard this had all been on her. The files all contained pictures of the dead women and Ricki's file was a part of the stack. Johni had read through every part of the file on Ricki and then the one on Whitney. It was taxing on her; she could imagine what it must be doing to Johni. After hanging up with room service, Johni plopped back down onto the floor where they had been reading the files.

"Are you okay?" Raven asked. Johni favored her with a smile.

"I'm okay. It's just that all this," she answered sweeping her arm out over the files on the floor between them, "why? Why do all this? What reason could a person possibly have to kill sixteen people?"

"I know." Raven agreed.

"You know what else amazes me? Whoever is doing it is good. There's not one clue to indicate who is doing this and what's even more amazing is that no one saw a thing."

"You would think that someone would have seen something." Raven added. Johni was about to say something else when there was a knock at the door. Raven watched as she answered it and accepted the drinks from the room service attendant. She tipped him and turned to sit down again. After a couple of sips on the Morgan's and Pepsi she'd ordered Johni picked up the file on Ricki again.

"It says here that there were indications of a struggle at the top of the Leap this time. Why,..." The phone rang and Johni reached over her head to answer it.

"Hello?" She said into the phone. Raven watched her face for an indication of who it might be. Considering that they were here she worried that it might be one of the kids or something. Johni teased her that she was a compulsive worrier. After a couple of moments recognition set into Johni's face. "Detective Greyson, yes how are you?" Raven got up and went into the bathroom. She was washing her hands when she heard Johni say good-bye and hang up the phone. Johni appeared in the bathroom behind her.

"That was Greyson." She offered hugging Raven from behind. Raven leaned back into her. "He is coming by with someone from the local Gay and Lesbian Alliance, the leader of the local chapter I think. He thinks she might help. I told him not to tell her what we are doing but instead that we are interested in getting married here."

"Why not just tell her?" Raven asked slipping by Johni. If someone was coming over they needed to pick up this mess.

"Well, the less people to know the better, besides that's the only way to ensure that no one gets wind of what we are doing. This will be a great way to get the word out that we are here and going to get married." Raven nodded to indicate that she agreed with Johni's logic and continued to pick up. Married. There was a big part of her that wished it were true. She could just imagine what it would be like to be able to consider herself Johni's wife. Sure they had lived together for a while now and they paid their bills together and all but being married, that was different. That was a big commitment. She knew that Johni would do it in a minute but she was still skittish. She had to be sure that it was the right thing to do. The sad thing was that even the kids had approached her about it. Dionne had been all for it from the start and although it took Kevin a little time to warm up he too was now willing to walk his mom down the aisle. She was the only hold out. It was a shame. She finished picking up while Johni gathered the police files and put them away. Just as they finished there was another knock at the door. This time it was Raven who answered. She was surprised to find a tall thin brunette standing on the other side. She had expected someone who looked more local.

"Ms. Andrews?" The woman asked. Her voice was husky. It didn't fit her face or body at all. It reminded Raven of Kathleen Turner.

"No, I'm Raven Michaels, please come in Ms....?"

"Noel Tanner. Pleased to meet you Ms. Michaels."

"Raven, please." She walked into the room and stopped just inside the door for Raven to take the lead. Raven smiled and lead her into the room where Johni was. "Ms. Tanner,"

"Noel please." The woman requested. Raven nodded.

"Noel, this is my other half, Johni Andrews." Johni stepped forward and offered her hand. Raven watched carefully to see if there was any reaction in Johni to Noel Tanner. Satisfied that there wasn't she offered Noel a chair. She then took the seat next to Johni and Johni laid a hand territorially on her leg.

"I understand you two are going to be getting married

on the island." Noel started. She gets to the point, Raven thought, I like that.

"Yes we are." Raven answered with a smile. "Detective Greyson thought you'd be able to help."

"Are you friends of the Detectives?" The woman asked politely.

"Through a mutual friend," Johni said shifting in her seat. "What kinds of services are available here?"

"There are a lot of different options." Noel started. "You can marry on the beach, a boat, in the jungle, wherever your preference is. Many of our weddings are held on the beach needless to say but our island is at your disposal."

"Are their special preparations we need to go through concerning the new rules?" Johni was on a fishing trip so Raven sat back to let her go.

"Only one...that you register with the local Gay and Lesbian Alliance chapter, and also with the island hall of records. For every marriage that takes place it's one more notch in the belt of equal rights." Johni nodded and turned to Raven.

"Is there anything you'd like to ask Doc?" Raven thought for a moment. At the moment she was blank.

"Can we have your phone number in case we have questions later?"

"Of course," Noel said pulling a card from her bag.

"Here's my card, call anytime." Raven took the card and looked it over quickly. Nothing to write home about. She smiled her thanks and stood up. Their visitor followed suit as did Johni.

"Thank you for coming over, we will be in touch." Raven said offering her hand.

"You're welcome." Noel said walking to the door, "I'd like to invite the two of you to my home for dinner. The address is on the card and any local can tell you how to get there. It's tomorrow night. Please come and join us, it'll give you a chance to meet some of the other locals."

"We'll do that." Johni said reaching to open the door. Noel said good-bye one more time and left. Johni closed the door and went back to where she was sitting.

"What do you think?" Raven asked taking a seat across from her.

"Well having to register in two separate places certainly gives a killer two places to pull names from."

"I think so too. We need to find out if the others registered and if so how soon before their deaths." Raven offered.

"I'll call and get Greyson on it." Johni said reaching for the phone. Raven sipped her spritzer and waited for Johni to finish the call. When she hung up Johni turned back to her with a grin on her face.

"I guess you already have a fan huh?"

"What are you taking about?" Raven asked innocently.

"Noel Tanner. Don't sit here and try and tell me you didn't notice that she was checking you out." Johni teased.

"According to you everybody checks me out." Raven sniffed. "I don't even know when to take you seriously anymore. Johni got up from her chair and kneeled down before Raven's chair.

"I check you out all the time." Johni crooned pushing up to kiss her on the chin. "I just assume that everyone else does too." Raven laughed and swatted Johni on the top of the head.

"Very funny. So what do we do now?"

"Well," Johni said sitting back on her heels, "I guess the next logical thing to do is plan a wedding."

"Oh I'm sure you're going to love that." Raven said sarcastically.

"I can only hope that all of this wedding stuff will help to push you along." Johni added getting up. Raven felt bad. She wished that she could just do it. Andi had really scarred her. She followed Johni outside on the balcony and caught her from behind.

"One of these days." She offered.

"Yeah, I guess I'll just have to wait." Johni answered in a faraway voice. Raven stood holding onto her. The island breezes had picked up slightly. She could smell the salt in the air. She held on tightly to Johni.

"It won't be forever." She whispered in Johni's ear. Johni squeezed her arm.

"I'd still wait if it was Doc." She said quietly. Raven held on tighter. She knew Johni meant what she was saying. She would wait forever. Raven had no doubt.

Chapter 13

Raven sat looking out over the ocean in awe of the garden like atmosphere around them. They had woke early this morning determined to play the impending marriage thing to the hilt. Nothing could have prepared her though for the restaurant Johni had chosen for breakfast. It was right on the beach in an area called Telefofo Falls on the west side of the island. It was beautiful. They had driven the ten minute drive from the hotel around the coast of the south end of the island. The route had been the most scenic Raven had ever seen with high cliffs, restless seas and lush vegetation. She had marveled at the vivid colors of the plants and the sea. She'd never seen so many shades of blue. Johni had explained hat the further you go out to sea the deeper the blues. Even from the road they could follow the blues out into the ocean. When they arrived at the Garden Falls restaurant Raven had to fight to keep her chin from hitting the ground. It was incredible. The parking lot gave way to an immense arch that was covered with some sort of creeping vine. Once through the arch they found themselves at the foot of a huge water fall. The falls drained into a pool at the base of a cliff. Surrounding the pool were tables for patrons. It was as if the restaurant itself was a part of the falls. They were lead to a table close to the pool and Raven was amazed that they didn't get wet. The spray from the falls was immense but it wasn't until they were right up at the tables that they realized that the falls were so big that they gave off the illusion of being closer than they actually were. The tables had been place well out of the range of the falls. They took their seats and Johni ordered for them. Raven waited until the waiter had left before she expressed her delight.

"Johni this place is incredible."

"I know." Johni said with a smile. "It's one of my favorite places."

"I can see why." Raven looked around in wonder at how the restaurant was constructed. It had a Polynesian atmosphere with lots of lush plants and large wooden totems that supported a roof made mainly of bamboo. A stream ran along the outside from the falls into the ocean. It was cool and the ocean breezes flowed through the interior. The smell of the oceans salt water mixed nicely with the aroma of island foods that flowed from the kitchen. A bar ran the length of one side of the restaurant while the view of the water fall also offered a view of the ocean. Raven was still scanning the restaurant when Johni's smiling face came into view.

"What?" Raven asked self-consciously.

"You like it here huh?"

"Yes, it's wonderful." Raven said again. She was gushing and she hated that.

"So what do you think of this as a sight for a wedding?"

"What?" Raven asked surprised. Johni continued to smile. She is serious, Raven finally decided.

"Well?" Johni asked again. Raven was about to answer when a waiter appeared with their food. He served them wished them well and took his leave. Raven almost forgot what they were talking about. The food smelled delicious and looked heavenly. And there was so much of it. One thing about the people of this island they believed in feeding you. She didn't know where to start. Looking up at Johni she had to smile.

"I don't know where to start." She said putting voice to her thoughts. Johni laughed.

"Anywhere you'd like but while you're at it please tell me what you think of having the wedding here?" Johni asked again. Raven looked around again considering.

"It's beautiful." She remarked, then looking back at Johni she smiled. "I think that would be wonderful." Johni smiled broadly, proud.

"Great! Wait until you taste the food." She said driving into her own plate. Raven followed suit sampling each thing before getting serious about eating. It was a habit she'd formed over the years. Johni often teased her about it. They ate in silence for a time and then when she finally felt like stopping long enough to say anything Raven sat back and sighed.

"This is wonderful. If I'm not careful I'll pop."

"I know," Johni agreed sitting back, "Me too."

"So what's next?" Raven asked poking her fork into her food. Johni grinned and she stopped. "What?"

"That's a sure sign that you've had enough to eat." Johni said indicating Raven's plate. "You're playing in your food." Raven frowned and then put the fork down. Damn, she thought, she watches everything.

"Am not." Raven protested half heartily. "So what's next?"

"I guess we need to go down and register at the alliance and the island hall of records." Raven sighed.

"I hate to leave here." She said indicating the falls. Johni nodded.

"I know what you mean." They sat a half hour longer sipping iced coffee and talking about their trip so far. Finally, reluctantly Johni paid the bill and they left the restaurant.

"I guess we should start with the Hall of Records." Johni offered buckling her seat belt.

"Fine with me." Raven agreed. "But this afternoon we need to do some shopping." Johni put the key in the ignition and started the car.

"Shopping for what?"

"Clothes." Raven answered absently. Johni looked at Raven perplexed.

"What?"

"You heard me clothes, I need something to wear tonight to the party."

"You have got to be kidding." Johni said putting the car into gear. "All of those suitcases and you don't have anything to wear? Impossible!" Raven smiled sweetly at Johni. Poor girl, Raven thought, just don't know a lot about feminine women do you.

"I need something new to wear to the party."

"Why?" Johni persisted.

"Because, I don't want the first impression everyone at the party has of me to be that I didn't take the time to buy something new, besides I don't have anything island oriented." Raven explained. Johni pulled out onto the main road and sighed heavily.

"I don't understand you at all sometimes." She said sarcastically. Raven laughed and leaned over kissing her cheek.

"That's okay dear, you're not supposed to." Johni mockingly pulled away and grunted.

"Women!"

"Yeah, but you love me." Raven stated confidently. Johni looked over at her and Raven smiled. She couldn't help but laugh and after a moment Raven joined in too.

* * *

The Hall of Records was a newly built building in downtown Agana. It hadn't taken long to find and unlike many big city Records buildings it was just about empty. Johni walked straight to the desk.

"We need to register to be married." She told the lady behind the desk. The woman appeared to be a local. She was short as were many of the islands Chammaros and she had a sort of built in friendliness. She smiled as she handed a small packet of paperwork to Johni with a pen and indicated a table where she could fill out them out. Johni immediately turned and handed the papers to Raven. When they were seated at the table Raven leaned forward.

"Why do you do that?" She asked slightly annoyed.

"Do what?" Johni asked absently scanning the room.

"Walk in acting like you're taking care of things only to turn around and hand me the work." Raven answered as she started filling out the papers. She looked up to see Johni looking at her as if she were speaking another language. She shook her head and continued to fill out the paperwork. "Never mind," she gave up. She had very few complaints about her relationship with Johni however one that was apparent a lot of the time was Johni's need to be in control. It was annoying. She seemed determined that anyone who saw them together realize that she was the more controlled of the two of them. Normally this wouldn't have bothered her except for Johni's need to be consistent about it. There was hardly ever a time when Johni would let her take the lead, many times she would have to force her way to the front. They had discussed it many times and every time Johni would apologize and promise to try and change. Needless to say it never happened. She had resigned herself to the fact that Johni was young and maybe as she got older she would settle in enough to change that and a few other annoying youthful habits. She finished the paperwork and instead of handing it back to Johni she took it back to the counter herself. As she did Johni appeared slightly annoyed but then seemed to let it go. One more victory for you, Raven thought as she stood waiting for the lady behind the counter to look over her answers.

"So you've come to the island to marry?" The woman asked.

"Yes we did." Raven answered with a smile. The woman smiled back and then continued to go over the papers.

"I see that you are from Seattle, is it nice there?"

"We like it." Johni answered impatiently. Raven shot her a hard look to stop her from saying anything further. Johni shrugged her shoulders and walked away.

"You'll have to forgive my partner," Raven offered, "She's a little on edge. We were told last night that another couple committed suicide a couple of days ago."

"Were they friends of yours?" The woman seemed genuinely concerned.

"Oh no, it's just unnerving when someone in your community does something so horrible." Raven whispered. The woman nodded her understanding.

"I understand that not everyone believes that they did it to themselves." The woman offered in a conspiring whisper. Raven leaned forward feigning surprise.

"Really?"

"Yes, there are rumors of other deaths too." She added quickly. "They say.." The woman suddenly fell silent. Raven looked up to see that a man had entered the office from behind her and was now favoring the woman with a stern look of reproach. Raven took her queue.

"Is that all we need to do?" She asked a little louder than before.

"Yes mam," the woman answered gratefulness in her eyes. "Now you may want to register with the islands Gay and Lesbian Alliance in Dededo." Johni who had been keeping her distance now appeared at Raven's side.

"Is that on the main strip in Dededo?" She asked. The woman nodded.

"It's next to Chang's Fish Market on Carnation Street."

"I know of Chang's." Johni assured her. "Thank you."

"You're welcome. Enjoy our island and good luck with your marriage." The woman said smiling.

"Thank you, I'm sure we'll have a wonderful time if everyone is just half as nice and helpful as you." Raven said taking her hand and giving it a squeeze. She could see that the man who'd come in earlier was watching the exchange carefully. The woman gave Raven a grateful wink and Raven winked back. She and Johni left. Once out the door Johni touched Raven's arm gently.

"What was that all about?"

"Nothing," Raven answered, "Just one woman helping another." Johni thought about it and then appeared to let it go. Raven smiled to herself as she glanced back at the building. It was always nice to help someone else.

* * *

The registration at the Gay and Lesbian Alliance wasn't much different except that they piled literature about the islands gay community's activities. The party at Noel Tanner's was mentioned again and they let the woman behind the desk know that they had already been invited. They stood up ready to leave when the young woman who'd taken their paperwork cleared her throat.

"Do you mind if I ask you a question?" She requested politely. You already have, Raven thought with a smile, then out loud she added,

"Not at all."

"Why did you choose Guam?" Raven hesitated for a

moment and Johni answered the woman.

"A friend suggested it." The woman smiled.

"I see. Well if we can be of any assistance please let us know."

"Thank you." Johni answered and they left the building. On the way back to the car Johni seemed thoughtful.

"What's up?" Raven asked.

"Nothing really, just thinking about the other couples, coming to start a life only to have someone take their dreams from them."

"I know." Raven agreed taking Johni's arm. She shivered slightly and couldn't tell if it was a result of the conversation or if a breeze had chilled her momentarily. She was looking down when she felt Johni step in front of her slightly. Looking up she saw what was making Johni cautious. Sitting on the hood of their rental car was a woman. As they got closer the woman didn't move. She was a Black woman who looked like she might be in her late forties. Her face was weathered and hardened. A cigarette hung loosely from her lips. When they stopped just short of the car the woman slid off the hood and removed the cigarette.

"Hell I didn't think you two were ever going to finish." She said loudly. Johni and Raven looked at each other and then back to the woman.

"Do we know you?" Johni asked moving Raven just a

touch more behind her again.

"Well no I don't imagine you do." The woman answered with a laugh.

"Okay, then who are you and why are you sitting on our car?" Johni asked slightly annoyed now.

"I am your connection; your own personal island guide." The woman boasted.

"We don't need a guide." Johni said sternly.

"Oh, but I think you do." The woman insisted with a smile. "Names Grady, Grady Peaks." She offered her hand to Johni who hesitated and then shook it carefully. "Why don't we go get out of the sun and talk? There's a little bar up the street." Johni looked at Raven who shrugged and nodded.

"Why not?" Johni looked at the woman again.

"Okay." She stood back for the woman to lead the way, Raven behind her. Raven smiled. Johni made her feel so protected at times. They arrived at the bar in less the two minutes. It was a seedy little place. It was dark and smelled of stale beer. They took a table near the door, Johni sitting between Raven and Grady Peaks.

"What's this all about?" Johni asked as soon as the waitress delivered three beers. Raven sipped hers knowing she wouldn't finish it. Peaks leaned forward.

"I understand you're getting hitched."

"And?" Johni pushed.

"And I understand that you may be interested in certain murders here on the island in recent times as well." Raven looked at Johni who was having a hard time controlling her surprise.

"Who are you?" Johni asked sternly.

"A friend," Peaks answered taking a long draw from her beer.

"Why do we need a friend?" Johni asked suspicious. Peaks smiled.

"Things on this island aren't exactly what they seem Andrews. Careful is the word here." Peaks answered.

"How do you know my name?" Johni demanded. Peaks laughed.

"Ain't much around here I don't know. You two may be getting into something you can't handle."

"Like what?" Raven asked breaking her silence for the first time.

"Like here on this island your friends might not always be your friends Raven." Peaks answered quietly. The sound of the woman using her name made Raven jump slightly. "You two better watch yourselves. There's no telling what's lurking around in the shadows around here." Peaks stopped speaking abruptly as two men came in and took a seat at the bar. She seemed suspicious of the two new arrivals. "I have to go to the little girls room. I'll be right back." Peaks got up and went through a door at the back of the bar. Raven noticed how the two men at the bar watched her.

"Johni what's going on?"

"I don't know but I'm damn sure going to find out." Johni got up and went through the same door Peaks had gone through. A couple of minutes later she emerged and walk directly to the table. Dropping a couple of dollars onto the table she took Raven's arm and lead her out of the bar. Without saying a word they walked to the car quickly. Once in the car Johni started the engine and took off out of the parking lot as fast as she dared. As they passed the bar the two men that had been sitting at the bar emerged looking rather annoyed.

"Johni what happened to Peaks?"

"I don't know," Johni answered looking straight ahead. "There was no one in the bathroom but a small window in the back was open. It appears that she snuck out."

"But why?"

"My guess is that it had something to do with those two guys." Johni answered turning into the parking lot of the hotel.

"What's going on?" Raven asked suddenly filled with fear.

"I don't know Doc." Johni answered parking the car. "But I intend to find out."

Chapter 14

Johni stormed into the room and dropped the keys onto the bed as she picked up the phone. Raven had never seen her this irritated before. She was calling Greyson to find out who Peaks was. On the way up in the elevator she'd explained to Raven that she was not going to allow her to be put in any danger. Although Raven found this endearing she was also slightly annoyed with the concept of her not being given credit for being able to take care of herself. She was perfectly capable of handling just about anything, a fact that she pointed out to Johni frequently in the past and again reminded her of on the way up. Johni, however hadn't appeared to be listening. Raven decided to just let her go. Once she had something in her head to do there was really no stopping her anyway. Johni angrily punched the keypad on the phone. Raven turned slightly so that Johni wouldn't see the smile growing across her face. Johni could really be dramatic when she was being territorial. Raven went out onto the balcony but stayed within ear shot. She listened as Johni got Greyson on the phone.

"Greyson? This is Johni Andrews. We had an incident this afternoon and I wanted to make you aware of it as well as ask some questions." Johni explained to the Detective what had happened at the Gay and Lesbian

Alliance and then at the bar afterwards. When she was finished there was silence on Johni's end. Raven surmised that the detective was telling Johni what she needed to know.

"So there's no danger from this woman?" Johni was confirming. Silence again and then Johni thanked the detective and hung up. She came out and joined Raven on the balcony.

"Well?" Raven asked as Johni took a seat next to her.

"It appears that Peaks is harmless." Johni confirmed her suspicions.

"I thought so." Raven said laying her head back. "So who is she?"

"Greyson says she's a local. She is apparently a lesbian but not part of the local community. Greyson says she's quite outspoken about the way the Alliance handles it's affairs." This piece of information caught Raven's attention.

"Really? Why?"

"Greyson doesn't know we'll have to ask Peaks if we ever run across her again. Greyson says she's always stirring up trouble though." Johni added.

"I'd like to talk to her again." Raven commented. "She seemed to want to tell us something." Johni appeared to be considering for a moment.

"She did at that." She agreed. "I wonder if Peaks

knows anything of use. Greyson says she has an uncanny ability to get information. He says she won't talk to him about any of it though. It appears she doesn't trust the cops."

"Can you blame her?" Raven asked with a hint of disgust in her voice. It was a known fact that the police departments around the planet weren't sympathetic to Gay and Lesbian causes. Why should Guam be any different?

"No not really. But maybe she'll tell us what she knows." Johni considered.

"Great but how do we find her?"

"I have a feeling that Ms. Peaks will find us when she's ready." Johni said getting up. "In the meantime it's almost two and we have some shopping to do." Raven looked at her watch.

"Two?!" She exclaimed. "I'll never be ready in time!" Johni started laughing. "What?" Raven asked annoyed.

"You," Johni answered pulling Raven to her feet and gathering her into her arms. "You don't need to go through all that trouble, you're beautiful just the way you are." Raven smiled and snuggled into Johni.

"Thank you honey but you love me so naturally you feel that way, I have to take these pains for those in the world who don't see what you see when you look at me."

"Ha, I'll bet I can find ten people who would agree with me right now." Johni challenged. Raven laughed, she knew that if she egged her on Johni would go look for those supposed ten people too.

"That's quite all right." She said laughing, "I trust you."

"Well," Johni stepped back and dramatically swung her arm towards the door. "Are you ready to shop until I drop?"

"Until you drop?" Raven questioned.

"Until I drop my dear, I'm quite certain you would never drop shopping." Johni teased. Raven slapped her on the arm and pointed to the door.

"Out you beast." She bellowed. Johni laughed and headed out the door.

* * *

They spent the better part of the day shopping the boutiques on the island. Raven not only bought new clothes for herself but also talked Johni into a new outfit. Finally having finished they headed back to the hotel and got dressed. It always took Raven roughly an hour and a half to get dressed so Johni would take a shower first and then patiently wait while Raven did her thing. She was grateful for Johni's patience. They were supposed to be at the party around seven so of course at seven-thirty she was finished. She had purchased an island wrap. It was beautiful with blues and reds and it fit Raven snug enough to accent her shape but not so much that it was uncomfortable. She had purchased Johni a shirt in the same pattern. When she came out of the bathroom she could see by the look on Johni's face that she'd done well.

"You like?" She fished. Johni grinned broadly.

"I like." Johni got up from her seat and took Raven into her arms. "You look like my very own island princess. How am I going to keep the other horny islanders off you?" Raven laughed.

"I guess you'll just have to trust me." Raven teased.

"Famous last words," Johni responded putting a hand over her heart.

"Well? Are you ready?" Raven asked seriously. Johni looked at her incredulously.

"Am I ready?"

"Yes, come on we're already late." Raven said as if the fact that they were late was Johni's fault.

"Why you little...." Johni said giving her a slight nudge towards the door.

"Hey!" Raven feigned annoyance.

"I'll hey you woman! Out!" Johni demanded pointing to the door. Raven mock pouted and went through the door. Johni laughed, shaking her head as she locked the room door behind them.

* * *

Noel Tanners home was exquisite. It was gated and a

guard looked for their names on a list as they drove in. Johni and Raven were impressed as they drove through the grounds to the main house.

"What a spread?" Johni commented as they drove the circular driveway. Raven didn't say anything but nodded her agreement. "I wonder what Noel Tanner does for a living?" Johni added. The main house was brightly lit. Music emanated from within and people were milling around both outside and on a second floor balcony that ran the length of the house. Johni pulled the car around and a young man in a red coat opened Raven's door, offering his hand to help her out. Raven took the young man's hand and then stepped back while Johni handed him the keys and took the ticket the young man was offering.

"Impressive." Raven said as the young man drove their car away.

"Showy." Johni corrected. They moved into the foyer of the house. The room beyond was massive and at first glance appeared to have been decorated with the 90's in mind. The furniture was obviously expensive and tastefully chosen. A Persian rug adorned the foyer and several waiters milled through the crowd of people offering glasses of what looked to be champagne. As they entered the room one of them brought a tray to them and offered them glasses which they both took graciously.

"I wonder where our hostess is," Johni asked. As if

she'd heard the question Noel Tanner appeared from their right.

"Raven, Johni, I'm glad you made it." Noel offered. "Did you find us okay?"

"We did just fine, thank you." Johni said offering her hand. Noel took it with a smile and then turned to Raven. "How are you this evening Raven?"

"Fine, thank you." Raven answered moving a bit closer to Johni. "It was nice of you to have invited us."

"Well, please feel free to mingle. The food is on the patio and drinks are just about everywhere. If I can get you something please feel free to ask." Noel offered.

"Thank you." Raven said again and with that Noel Tanner disappeared into the crowd. Johni and Raven stood for a minute and then looked at each other.

"Food?" Johni asked.

"Yes." Raven answered and they made their way through the crowd towards the open patio on the other side. The patio was beautiful. Noel had it decorated with lawn lanterns and flowers of every kind. The back of the house opened up to a beach. It was wonderful. A slight breeze had started. Johni and Raven found a table and sat down to eat. The food, obviously catered was terrific.

"You want another glass of champagne?" Johni asked. Raven considered for a moment. She wasn't a big drinker so alcohol tended to hit her quickly.

"Are you trying to get me drunk?" Raven asked coyly.

"Of course," Johni laughed.

"Sure one more won't hurt." Raven answered. Johni excused herself and went to find a waiter. Raven was enjoying the island breezes when a person suddenly sat down across from her. The quick movement startled her. The woman seated across from her was beautiful. She was slender, Raven guessed in her mid-thirties. She looked a little like Jodie Foster only her hair was light brown. This could get me into trouble, Raven thought to herself.

"May I help you?" She asked politely. The woman smiled.

"I know a beautiful lady like yourself is not here alone." The woman stated frankly. Raven felt herself blushing a little.

"Well no, I'm here with my girlfriend." Raven offered.

"And were might she have gone off too?" The newcomer questioned. "I know I wouldn't have left you alone." Raven smile in spite of the awkward situation.

"She went to get me something to drink, Ms.......?"

"Rona." The woman answered. "Rona Duncan. And you are?"

"Raven Michaels. Nice to meet you Rona, are you a friend of Noels?" Raven inquired.

"Isn't everyone?" Rona answered with a laugh.

"I don't know we just met her." Raven answered. She

searched for Johni trying not to be obvious.

"What brings you to Guam Ms. Raven?" Rona asked leaning forward.

"We're getting married." Johni's stated from behind Rona. It made the woman jump. Her voice was purposely lowered. Raven smiled slightly, Johni was getting territorial again. The woman jumped up.

"I'm sorry did I get your seat?" She stammered. Johni looked over the woman's shoulder at Raven. Seemingly satisfied that Raven was fine, Johni smiled.

"No not at all, And you are?"

"Rona Duncan." The woman offered her hand which Johni took firmly.

"Johni Andrews." Johni responded. Raven smiled to herself. It was nice to know she was still worth haggling over.

"Welcome to the island." Rona offered. "So you're getting married huh? That's great."

"Please sit back down." Johni said placing Raven's drink in front of her. She sat down as well making sure to reach for Raven's hand.

"Are you registered and all that?" Rona asked politely.

"Yes, today." Raven spoke up. "Everyone was extremely nice."

"Yeah we have a great bunch of people here." Rona commented. "So where are you going to do it at?"

"We were thinking of the beach, maybe at the Falls." Johni chimed in. At first Raven was surprised that Johni was giving away information she usually wasn't so open but one look into Johni's eyes and a wink told Raven that Johni was putting the word out. She fell into step talking excitedly about the Falls and such. It turned out that Rona was a very nice woman despite her original intentions. They sat and talked for a while and as people passed the table Rona took the liberty of introducing them to Johni and Raven. Most of the women were nice with the exception of a few hard core ones with little to say. There were always a few in every crowd. After a while the three of them moved back into the main house where the music was playing and people were dancing.

"Would you like to dance Doc?" Johni asked starting to move to the music. Raven smiled.

"Do you think they can handle it?" She asked indicating the crowd. Johni laughed.

"Come on." She said taking Raven's hand and excusing them from Rona's company. The two of them took the dance floor and sure enough after three dances people were watching them. Raven truly enjoyed it. She knew that she and Johni fit extremely well together. They had a natural combined rhythm. People always gave them room on the dance floor. They danced two more songs before stopping. When they did several people clapped. Sitting back down Raven snuggled close to Johni.

"I love you." She whispered. Johni put an arm around her.

"I love you too." She said kissing Raven's nose. The music ended abruptly and Noel Tanner stood on the stairs above the room with a microphone in her hand. She was waiting for the crowd to be quiet. When they were Noel turned the microphone on and spoke into it.

"I hope you are all having a good time." She offered and a small cheer rippled through the crowd. "Good. I want to welcome you all to my home. It's nice to see so many friendly faces. I want to take a moment to introduce you all to two newcomers to our island. You may have had the pleasure of watching them dance a few minutes ago. Johni, Raven, would you stand up please. Raven looked at Johni who was blushing. They stood. "This is Johni Andrews and Raven Michaels, they will be getting married soon on our beautiful island so I want you all to take a moment and welcome them." Then turning to Raven and Johni, Noel made a grand gesture with her hand. "Welcome to Guam Raven and Johni, may your days be long and your nights be peaceful." She toasted, a cheer went up and everyone took a sip of their drinks. "Now let's have some music!" Noel bellowed. Johni and Raven sat back down.

"That was nice," Johni solemnly.

"Yes it was now everyone knows we are getting married." Raven commented happily. She stopped short when she saw the look on Johni's face as she scanned the room. "What's the matter Johni?"

"You're right, now everyone knows, maybe even the killer." Johni commented. Raven felt the exhilaration of the earlier moment slip away. She hadn't considered that. She watched as Johni searched the faces in the room. A chill ran down her spine and the reality of what they were doing sank back in. They were bait. She looked up at Johni and saw concern and for the first time since they'd found Ricki's body Raven felt fear.

Chapter 15

Raven woke to the sound of running water. She cleared her eyes and reached over absently for Johni. The other side of the bed was empty. Sitting up on her elbows she listened and realized that the running water had been the shower. Glancing at the clock she was surprised to see that it was already after nine. She rarely stayed in bed this long; in fact, she was usually up before Johni. Raven laid back into the pillows. It must have been the champagne. She had never held alcohol very well which was why she made it a point not to drink much. She hadn't been drunk last night but she had felt relaxed. They had come back to the hotel after the party and fallen right to sleep. It had been a long day. Now she felt rested and from the bathroom she could hear Johni humming softly, she must have slept well too. Sitting up Raven swung her feet to the floor. Outside the sun shone brightly and if she strained just a little she could hear the waves coming in at the bottom of the cliffs outside their window. This was a lovely place. She had listened to Johni speak of it often but now that she was here it was much more than she could have imagined. The beach, the vegetation, the food, the sunsets, all of it was wonderful and sharing it all with Johni had made it that much better. Johni. Raven felt a warmth in her soul. Johni was so good to her. She was patient and kind. She had her faults but all in all Johni was a very special person. Johni's humming got a little louder and Raven smiled. She got up and walked to the bathroom door. Inside she saw the silhouette of Johni's body through the shower door. She felt a tingling between her legs. Quietly she slid the shower door open and stepped inside. Johni was washing her hair, eyes closed. She didn't realize Raven had joined her. Raven stepped up and slid her arms around Johni.

"Hey!" Johni said eyes still closed. "My girlfriend wouldn't like this."

"Oh yeah," Raven replied quietly, "well she'll never find out." Raven kissed Johni's chest and then moved to her mouth kissing her full and deep. Johni responded instantly gathering Raven up and kissing her back hungrily. They stood letting the water wash over them while they continued to explore each other's bodies with hands and mouths. Raven felt the heat from within her rise. It never ceased to amaze her how intense her feelings for Johni were. She could tell by John's responses that she felt the same. Raven stopped suddenly and pushed away from Johni.

"Hey, where do you think you're going?" Raven gave her a seductive grin and sat down on the shower bench along the wall. The shower was huge with enough room for four or more people. She laid back on the bench.

"You want me?" She said seductively, "Come get me." Johni let out a low groan and swiftly kneeled down in front of the bench. Raven turned to face her and put her arms around Johni's shoulders. Johni buried her face into Raven's chest and quickly found her breasts with her mouth. Raven let out a moan and threw her head back as Johni worked her nipples over with her mouth. Raven grabbed the back of Johni's head and burrowed her fingers into her hair. She moved rhythmically as Johni moved from her nipples to her stomach. Excitedly Johni moved down even further until her mouth was on Raven's thighs.

"Oh Johni." Raven breathed, "You're so good to me." Her words seemed to excite Johni more as she kissed Raven's inner thighs. Johni stopped suddenly and pulled back for just a moment to let the tension build up. Raven opened her eyes and looked down at Johni who was breathing heavily.

"Tell me," Johni demanded. Raven squirmed at the thought of Johni was about to do.

"Please?" Raven requested quickly.

"What?" Johni asked blowing lightly on the heated mound between Raven's legs. The sudden breath on her most private of places goaded her into action. She grabbed Johni's head and pulled her towards her.

"Give me your tongue," Raven demanded. Eager to comply Johni quickly leaned into Raven letting her tongue roam free. She traced the lines and curves and explored every crevice in Raven's pulsating kitten. Raven responded moving with Johni and she rose and fell with each new thrust of Johni's tongue. Raven felt her muscles tighten and then with a gush her bush got wetter and wetter. She rode the waves of passion as Johni loved her with intensity like she'd never felt before. Suddenly she had to have Johni too. Pushing Johni away she quickly and quietly pulled Johni up and laid her down on the bench. Johni asked no questions but silently followed as if in a trance. Once Johni had lain down Raven straddled her in a position that would allow her to explore Johni with her tongue just as Johni did so to her. With a renewed eagerness Johni went back to work pleasuring Raven with her tongue. Raven spurred on by Johni's movements leaned into Johni as well and found her wet and willing to accept Raven's tongue. They moved together in time oblivious to the outside world. Raven tried to hold her rising organism so that she and Johni could come together and just when she felt that she would no longer be able to hold it she felt Johni reaching hers too. In an incredible moment of passion and desire both woman came together with such intensity that for a moment Raven thought that her heart might stop. Wave after wave of ecstasy washed over them as they held each other each waiting for the other to finish. After several minutes Raven finally found her voice.

"I have never," she breathed heavily, "felt like that before."

"Me either." Johni responded. They readjusted and sat together side by side on the bench holding one another. "I love you Raven."

"I love you too." Raven said kissing Johni's chin. After a few moments more they both stood and they showered together each washing the other gently. Afterwards when they had both toweled off and dressed they sat together on the balcony in silence. Johni looked out over the ocean. The faraway look in her eyes prompted Raven to inquire as to her thoughts.

"What are you thinking about?"

"Nothing really." Johni answered in a faraway voice.

"Try again."

"I use to think that I would never find someone to love me the way that you do." Johni explained. "I was just thanking God that I had." Raven smiled and reached over to squeeze Johni's hand.

"I never thought I would find anyone either."

"Guess we were both wrong." Johni offered.

"Thank God." Raven agreed.

* * *

They spent the rest of the day setting up their wedding

plans. They walked through the invitations, the cater; they even reserved the restaurant at the Falls. They spared no expense. Greyson had told them to go all out; the police department would be picking up the tab because the entire thing was to be staged as a sting operation. They picked out a dress for Raven and tuxes the whole nine yards.

"It's too bad this isn't for real." Raven whispered as they waited for Johni's tux. Johni smiled and nodded. Raven knew that Johni was indeed wishing that all of it was real. She felt a stab of guilt.

"Hungary?" Johni asked as she paid for the tux.

"Yes."

"How about the hotel restaurant?"

"Okay." Raven answered as they got into the rental car. The hotel restaurant was extremely nice and her stomach had been growling for over an hour now. They drove back to the hotel. As they pulled into a parking place Raven noticed a commotion near the entrance of the hotel. Johni had spotted it too.

"Wonder what's up?" Johni said setting the parking brake. They got out and walked cautiously toward the hotel entrance. Several police cars and an ambulance were parked at an angle that made it hard to see what was happening. Before Johni could stop her Raven stepped between the cars and was heading through the small crowd that had gathered. She struggled to keep up excusing herself through the crowd. When they reached the inner circle Raven gasped as she was confronted with what appeared to be a person hanging with a rope around its neck seemingly suspended from the hotel. It took a second for her to realize that it wasn't a person at all but a dummy made up to look like a person. Johni was at her side a split second later and Raven could tell by her reaction that she'd thought the same thing when she had first seen it. A group of policemen were standing near the sidewalk. Greyson was among them. He glanced up and when he realized that they were standing in the crowd he motioned to them to join him and the officers. Carefully side stepping the dummy Raven followed Johni over to Greyson.

"What's going on?" Johni asked Greyson.

"I was hoping you could tell us." Greyson responded looking back at the dummy.

"Us why?" Raven asked surprised. Greyson said nothing but rather pointed to the source of the rope tied to the dummy. Raven followed his finger and with a quick calculation saw the source of his question. If she had counted right, and she was sure she had, the other end of the rope was coming from a room on the eighth floor. Surprised she looked at Johni. From the look on her face she had drawn the same conclusion.

"Johni?" Raven said stepping closer to her.

"I know." Johni said not taking her eyes off of the room window. "That's our room."

Chapter 16

Greyson looked over the edge of the railing. Johni, standing next to him followed the rope from the balcony railing down to the make shift body dangling carelessly on the other end. Raven watched them both from inside the room and wondered how they could be so calm. Chills had run down her spine when she had first seen the dummy on the rope and realized that the other end had been tied off in their room. The chills had been beating a path up and down her spine ever since. Johni had remained remarkably calm from the start. The only change in her demeanor had been an increased effort to keep Raven close. Greyson stood up and wiped his brow. It appeared that this latest event had him concerned. He spoke to one of the officers dusting the balcony for finger prints and then motioned for Johni to follow him inside. They both came inside and Greyson took a seat opposite Raven. Johni sat down in the chair beside her. The look on both their faces was grave. She looked first at Johni and then the detective. Greyson cleared his throat and spoke directly to Raven.

"I won't blame you if you want to pull out."

"Out?" Raven couldn't help but find this concept ridiculous. "Now is not the time to bow out. Obviously we have someone's attention."

"This," Greyson said as two police officers brought the dummy in from the balcony, "is a clear threat. I can't ask you to continue after this. If you decide to stick it out it'll be entirely your decision." Raven looked at Johni for support and was surprised to see none.

"What about you?" She asked Johni more than a little annoyed. "You want to cut and run too?" She saw Johni flinch slightly. She knew that her words were cutting deep but it didn't stop her. She couldn't believe that everyone was bailing.

"Detective Greyson," Johni said ignoring Raven's question. "When will the test results from the dummy be in?"

"It'll be at least forty-eight hours, our lab is small but I will push for it as soon as possible. Why?" Johni looked at Raven in silence for a moment and then turned back to the detective. "We aren't quitting but I'd like as much information as we can get." The detective looked slightly surprised.

"Are you sure?"

"As sure as I can be." Johni sighed. "As you can see my fiancée isn't willing to give in yet." Greyson considered Raven for a moment and then shook his head.

"You are one brave lady." He told Raven as he got up from his seat.

"Not brave," Raven corrected. "I just don't like leaving

something half done." Greyson nodded and said his good-byes. Johni walked him and the last uniformed officer to the door.

"I am placing a man on the hotel." Greyson assured Johni. "If you need him call 911 and he'll be here immediately."

"Thank you." Johni said shaking the man's hand. Shutting the door she turned around slowly and the look on her face told Raven that she was in for a confrontation. Deliberately, Johni came over and sat down, not next to her but in the seat across from her. She fidgeted for a moment. Uh oh, Raven thought, I've gone a bit too far again. Periodically she would mouth off or say something flip that would make Johni annoyed. She didn't always mean to, she just couldn't help it. She was a strong personality and sometimes her mouth would just run. She tried to put on her best please-forgive-me smile and waited. Johni sighed at the sight of her smile.

"Raven, was that really necessary?" Johni asked the annoyance apparent in her voice. Raven quickly tried to think of a way out but her urge to fix it was quickly squelched when Johni rose from her chair and started to pace. She hated it when Johni paced, it made her feel like a little kid. Despite common sense, she felt herself getting defensive.

"You mean after that glowing show of support?" She

asked sarcastically. It didn't matter if Johni was upset now, she wasn't going to be talked to like she were a child. Johni stopped pacing and faced her.

"What the hell is that supposed to mean?" Johni asked very obviously annoyed now. Raven knew that if she used tone of voice right it would piss Johni off. It was one of the few ways that she knew she could get to her. For reasons Raven didn't know Johni was extremely sensitive to the way things were said. If she took the slightest sarcastic tone with her Johni would jump to assuming that Raven meant more than she did. Most times Johni was wrong in her assumptions but now and then Raven used this personality quirk to her advantage. It was wrong but hell, at times Johni just made her angry.

"You were ready to cut and run." Raven explained arrogantly. "At least I was prepared to see it through." Johni's complexion turned slightly red. Raven knew that she was getting a rise out of her and she knew that she should stop before she really went too far but she couldn't help herself. "I guess you don't care who killed Ricki." Oh God, Raven thought, what the hell did I say that for. Johni had started pacing again but Raven's words stopped her in her tracks.

"What?" She asked loudly. Raven knew that she should pull back, stop now but she was already committed and one of her biggest downfalls was that, as Walker use to say, she didn't know when to shut up.

"If you cared it would have not even occurred to you to pull out now but at the first sign of real trouble you want to give up. Honestly Johni I would think that you would need to see whoever killed Ricki caught." Johni was pissed now; she could see it in her eyes. She walked directly up to Raven and leaned down putting both hands on the arms of Raven's chair. Raven tried to put up a brave front and even though she knew that Johni would never hurt her she still was a little leery of the intensity of Johni's anger when she'd gone too far.

"You know nothing of how I feel about Ricki's death." Johni stated. She was dangerously calm. "I was thinking of your safety. If you could stop playing Nancy Drew for just a moment maybe you'd realize that whoever this killer is he or she just upped the ante." Johni stood up and drew in a breath. Raven could see in her eyes how angry she was. She turned and picked up the key card to the room. Raven's competitive spirit was crushed by fear but she still struggled to hide it.

"And where do you think you're going?" She demanded standing up. Johni looked up at her.

"I'm going down stairs to cool off."

"Oh that's just like you, get upset and leave.!" Raven said turning her back to Johni. She was trying to get Johni to stay and hash this out by provoking her. If this didn't work she have to try and think of something else. Oh why didn't she shut up before it went this far. When Johni didn't respond but instead went into the bathroom Raven started to panic. What now?

"So you're going to run from this too?" Raven blurted out. Five seconds after she said it a voice inside her head screamed no, no, no. Johni came out of the bathroom looking struck and went out the room door. With the closing of the door Raven sat down hard in her chair.

"Of all the stupid things to say." She said out loud to the empty room. She sat staring at the door trying to determine what to do next. She knew that Johni wouldn't go far, in fact she would go to the bar, have a couple of beers and cool off. Still, she couldn't help but feel hurt that Johni left; even if it was technically her fault. She would just have to go downstairs and apologize. Or she could just stay here and stew until Johni returned. She sighed heavily. If she stayed here by the time Johni came back she'd be mad and they'd just argue again. Deciding it best to go downstairs she went into the bathroom to freshen up. Satisfied with what she saw in the mirror she turned the light off. She was looking for the other key card when the phone rang. She smiled to herself as she picked up the phone, Johni just couldn't wait. She was sure that it was Johni calling to ask her to come down. She was wrong.

"Hello?" She answered sweetly.

"What a sweet voice." The caller commented. Instantly Raven realized that the voice on the other end of the phone was not Johni.

"Who is this?" Raven asked cautiously.

"Don't get your panties in a wad." The caller chuckled. Raven thought she recognized the voice from somewhere.

"Who is this?" She demanded again.

"Grady Peaks." The caller answered feigning hurt. "You mean I made that little an impression?" Warning bells sounded in Raven's mind. She wished Johni was here. She quickly regained her composure.

"Of course I remember you Ms. Peaks. What can I do for you?"

"First off you can call me Grady. I don't intend to be Ms. Peaks to anyone but the undertaker." Grady said with a laugh. Raven felt herself relaxing a little. "Second you can meet me so that I can talk to you about this mess you've gotten yourself into." Raven's warning system kicked off again.

"What are you referring to?" Raven asked carefully. On the other end of the phone Grady Peaks laughed again.

"I know about the investigation Raven as well as what happened at the hotel today. I just want to talk. Can you and your friend meet me at Roma's on Yigo Beach in half an hour?" Raven's mind reeled with possibilities. Could

Peaks be the killer? How did she know so much? In an instant she made the decision.

"Yes we can."

"Good, I'll be sitting in the back by the beach." Peaks confirmed. "I'll see you then. And Raven...."

"Yes?" Raven answered.

"I'm not your killer." Raven felt her heart beating in her throat. Peaks hung up and with the dial tone Raven felt a renewed sense of urgency. She had to find Johni.

* * *

The bar downstairs in their hotel was elegant. Although it wasn't huge it had a piano bar and the music was nice. Raven searched for Johni. She walked through first searching the tables for Johni's face. When she didn't see it she went to the bar and asked if anyone had seen her. The bartender stated that he had but she had left. Frustrated Raven left the bar and stood in the lobby trying to decide what to do next. She couldn't just not go talk to Peaks; she could have some information that might help them. Raven went to the front desk and quickly left a message for Johni telling her where she had gone. Johni probably had gone for a walk on the beach and frankly she didn't have time to wait. Thanking the desk clerk Raven raced out of the hotel to one of the cabs parked out front.

Chapter 17

Johni sat back down at the bar and ordered another beer. One thing about drinking that probably kept her from becoming an alcoholic was the fact that after two beers she had to go to the bathroom. It was annoying. She used to watch her friends in the Air Force drink until they fell over and never once go to the bathroom. It had always amazed her. The bar keep brought her beer. Three beers would be her limit tonight. Her aim in coming down here in the first place had not been to get drunk but to calm down. She would have never hit Raven but at times the woman could make her feel dangerously close to losing control. She loved Raven with all of her heart. She felt for Raven things she hadn't thought possible until she'd met Raven Michaels. They had a good relationship but like every couple they had their moments. Nothing drastic, just times when one or the other of them would say something that wasn't so nice. After all Raven wasn't the only one who could run her mouth right into trouble. Raven just had a special knack for it. Johni on the other hand was notorious for small acts of selfishness. She would do small things at times and completely disregard Raven. She didn't mean to of course but sometimes she just didn't put enough thought into things. Johni sighed. They both had their moments, that was for sure. Picking up her beer she drained half of it. She was replacing it on the bar when she noticed that the bar keep seemed to be hovering. She motioned for him to come over.

"Do I look like someone you know?" She asked casually. The young man was obviously a little taken aback by her forwardness. He recovered quickly though and smiled.

"I'm sorry I didn't mean to seem so obvious. A young woman was in here a couple of minutes ago looking for another woman and I was trying to figure out if you were the one she was looking for."

"What did she look like?"

"About thirty, maybe thirty-five, real looker." The young man answered. "Lady with a bright smile." Johni smiled. Thirty to thirty-five. Raven would have loved that. "Sound like someone you know?"

"Yeah, do you know where she went?" Johni asked looking around.

"Back towards the lobby," the bartender offered. "Hey," he said leaning over on the bar, "if you find her tell her there's a really nice guy in the bar who would love to buy her a drink." Johni smiled.

"I'll do that but you might have to take that up with her other half."

"Big guy huh?" The bartender asked looking disappointed. Johni laughed.

"That's funny, I've never been referred to as that before." She paid her bar bill as the young man stood and figured it out. When he did the look of surprise on his face was priceless. "See ya." Johni offered leaving. She walked into the lobby and did a quick search for Raven. When she didn't see her she headed for the elevator, half way there she heard someone call her name.

"Ms. Andrews," an Asian woman behind the hotel desk was calling to her, "Ms. Andrews I have a message for you." Johni turned and walked to the desk.

"A message? From who?" Johni asked taking a piece of paper from the woman. On the folded pink message sheet was a message from Raven.

Johni,
Looked for you but didn't see you.
Went to meet Grady Peaks at the Roma bar on Yigo Beach.
Raven

"Grady Peaks?" Johni said out loud.

"Excuse me?" The desk clerk asked.

"Nothing. When was this left?" Johni asked hurriedly.

"About twenty minutes ago." The young woman answered a look of concern on her face. "Is everything okay Ms. Andrews?" Johni took a moment to compose herself before responding.

"Yes, everything is fine." She answered calmly. "Did Ms. Michaels take a cab?"

"I'm not sure but Joe the doorman will know." Johni thanked the young woman and headed for the lobby door. She found Joe the doorman helping a little old lady into a cab. She waited as patiently as she could. When Joe was finished she asked if he'd seen Raven get into a cab. She described her and before she was finished Joe interrupted her with a smile.

"You are describing Ms. Michaels. A beautiful young lady," Joe offered. "She left about twenty minutes ago heading to Roma's on the beach."

"Thanks Joe." Johni said handing him a five. Joe waved it off. "Ms. Michaels is a wonderful lady, anything I can do to help. Would you like a cab?" Johni nodded and Joe waved for the nearest cab. Johni got in and Joe told the driver to take her to Roma's.

"Thanks Joe." Johni said again.

"No problem, give my best to Ms. Michaels."

"I will." Johni said as the cab pulled away. "How far?" She asked the driver.

"Ten minutes tops." He answered. Johni sat back and absently looked out the window. Raven, so impulsive. It scared her at times. The tone of her note was not one of anger so it was her guess that Raven went out of she deemed necessity. She still should have waited. What if Grady Peaks was the killer? Even as she thought Johni didn't believe that. Peaks didn't strike her as the killer type. Still, who were those men who were following her? If anything happened to Raven, Peaks would pay dearly. She should have not left Raven in the room in the first place. One of these days she was going to learn to control her temper, she admonished herself. She had always had that problem. When she was young a series of events had taught her distrust and anger in the worse way. Instead of being guided into life learning the skills essential to becoming a whole person she'd learned instead that she was alone. She had little to go on in the way of learning control coming from a place where little control had existed for her and the others in her life. She had yet to share her childhood with Raven and maybe she should, after all much of what had happened back then would help explain many of her reactions to things now. One day maybe, she thought. Looking at her watch Johni realized for the first time that the cab ride had already been more than ten minutes. She tapped on the plastic between herself and the driver.

"Hey, I thought you said ten minutes." The driver didn't respond but instead turned off of the main road into the parking lot of the harbor. With a few quick calculations Johni estimated that the harbor was at least two miles past where they were supposed to have gone. The hair on back of her neck stood straight up. She reached over and tried the door, it opened easily. The parking lot was dark and totally void of movement. Again she tapped on the plastic between herself and the driver.

"Hey!" She said loudly. "What are we doing here?" At first the driver didn't respond but as she started to hit the plastic window again he turned.

"Get out." He said calmly. His voice was deep and thick with an accent she didn't recognize.

"Excuse me?" Johni asked not bothering to try and hide the annoyance in her voice.

"Out!" The driver bellowed this time. Johni glanced around at the dark parking lot again.

"I don't think so." She said scooting over a little further into the seat. "Take me back to the hotel." Johni reached over and grabbed the door handle. Before she could pull the door shut it was wretched from her hand by an outside force. She tried to react but didn't move quick enough, a pair of hands grabbed her and she was hauled from the car. She heard voices but could see nothing in the darkness of the parking lot. She resisted but soon realized that it was a fruitless effort. Not one but two different sets of hands were on her now. She struggled to adjust her eyes to the darkness.

"What do you want?!" She shouted.

"Shut up!" A voice whispered off to her left. Oh, Johni thought quickly, so they want quiet eh?

"Let me go!" Johni shouted louder. "Help! Anybody!"

"Shut her up!" the same voice whispered furiously.

"Let me go!" Johni yelled again. "Let me go damn it!" Johni struggled harder and then suddenly she felt a hand over her mouth; a sweet smell filled her nostrils and her head started to spin. Oh damn she thought wildly, chloroform. She felt herself slipping to the ground and darkness crept in like a thief stealing what was left of her consciousness. The last thought Johni had before hitting the ground was of Raven. Who would protect Raven now?

Chapter 18

Raven stepped into Roma's and was impressed. The bar was literally on the beach. To get to the small parking lot you had to leave the main road and follow an unpaved road down to the beach. Once at the bottom of the hill, a sharp left brought you to the front door of Roma's. It was a quaint little place nestled between a group of palm trees and the sand of the beach itself. Roma's was what could be described as an open bar. The entire back side was open to the ocean. Raven walked to the bar and ordered a Morgan and Pepsi. The bartender was pleasant and several people sitting at the bar either said hi or nodded kindly. She knew she caught people's attention when she entered a room so it didn't bother her when she caught the leering glances of more than a few men. She paid for her drink and took it to a table right on the edge of the bar overlooking the beach. This is really nice, Raven thought sipping the rum and Pepsi. She watched the ocean as the waves rolled in and wished that Johni was here too. She hoped that she would get the message. She wouldn't want to worry her and she had hoped that she would get it in time to meet them here. A waitress suddenly appeared at the table with a fresh drink.

"I didn't order this." Raven said politely. The waitress smiled.

"It's from the woman at the bar." Raven looked back to see Noel Tanner tipping a beer her way.

"Please tell her I said thank you." Raven asked the waitress.

"Sure." The waitress answered. As she left Raven turned back to the beach. She was quietly praying that Noel didn't come over to join her. She wasn't sure that Grady Peaks would talk to her if someone else was there.

"Is this chair taken?" A voice from behind her asked. Damn! Raven thought and then turned with a smile. She was surprised to see that the voice belonged to Grady Peaks and not Noel Tanner. She glanced towards the bar. Noel wasn't anywhere in sight. Her surprise must have been apparent. "Expecting someone else?"

"What? Oh, no, I was actually trying to avoid someone and I had thought for a moment that I had failed." Raven said laughing. "Please, sit down." Grady sat down opposite Raven.

"Where's your friend?" Grady asked motioning to the waitress.

"She should be joining us anytime." Raven answered absently. She didn't want Grady to think that she'd come alone without benefit of Johni's company. After all she didn't know anything about Grady Peaks. Peaks ordered a beer. They small talk until it arrived. Peaks took one long draw off the beer and then turned serious.

"I'll bet your wondering why I asked you to meet me?"

"Well, yes." Raven answered. "It was a bit of a surprise after you disappeared the other day."

"Oh that. Yeah, well sorry; I had to lose those two goons." Peaks said sourly.

"Who were they?" Raven asked trying to sound as if she weren't actually prying.

"Cops." Peaks replied, then seeing the look on Raven's face she smiled. "Island cops who don't know anything about me except that I'm nosy."

"Did you do anything wrong?" Raven asked blatantly. Peaks laughed.

"You do believe in getting to the point don't you?"

"My mother taught me that if you wanted to know something, ask." Raven said grinning mischievously. Peaks laughed appreciatively.

"Your mother is right. And the answer is no." Peaks offered. "I have just managed to be here without the local police knowing a lot about me. I've been asking some uncomfortable questions." Raven's curiosity was aroused. She took a sip of her drink and asked her next question carefully.

"What sort of questions?" Peaks smiled and drained her beer. She called the waitress and ordered another one. When the waitress brought the second beer she sighed loudly.

"I have been on this island for three years now Raven." Peaks stopped and appeared to be reflecting quietly. After several moments she took another drink of her beer and seemed to return. She looked around as if to check out the scene and then leaned forward. "I am an FBI agent and I'm working on a case here on the island." Raven was skeptical.

"Why are you telling me?"

"You and your friend managed to land right in the middle of the case I'm working on." Peaks said quietly. "Oddly enough you seem to have gotten the attention of the killer where as I haven't in over three years of investigation." Raven still remained reserved; she needed to be sure she could trust Peaks. She wished desperately that Johni would show up. She must have gotten her message by now. Peaks interrupted her thoughts. "Here," she said pushing a small leather case over to her. Raven took the case and opened it. Inside was a shield and an identification card identifying Peaks as an FBI agent. It all looked real enough.

"Why aren't you working with the police department?" Raven asked. She had a million questions already.

"They may be involved in this mess." Peaks answered gravely. Raven was taken aback. The police? But they had been working for...she stopped short and for a moment felt her throat constrict.

"That's who asked us to work on this case."

"I know. I'm not positive that they are but there are a lot of holes in their investigations and the killer or killers seem to be able to easily evade them. Also there's the matter of my own personal police escort which, I might add, I picked up only after I started asking questions about the local police department." Peaks explained. Raven's mind reeled. The police? That would certainly explain why the killer hadn't been caught.

"Surely you don't suspect the entire police force?" Raven asked.

"No of course not but I have two that I would like to know more about." Peaks answered quietly. "Besides I think this transcends the department. I believe that there is more than one entity at work here."

"Like who?" Raven was getting far more involved in this conversation without Johni than she wanted to. She scanned the room again. Where could Johni be? She was about to turn back around when she noticed two men severely overdressed walk through the door. She recognized them from somewhere. She turned back to Peaks when she realized from where.

"Grady, those men from the bar the other day just walked in." She whispered.

"I see them." Peaks said hurriedly. "Raven, do you trust me?" Raven thought for a second and blurted out her answer.

"Yes."

"Come on then." Peaks said grabbing Raven's hand. They snuck out the back of the bar towards the beach. It was so dark Raven could hardly see. She stayed in step with Peaks trying to be sure of her footing. Peaks lead her expertly through the rocks and sand. After about five minutes they came out on a road. Panting they both looked around.

"What now?" Raven asked catching her breath.

"There's a convenience store over there." Peaks said pointing to a lighted store front about three blocks away. Let's get a cab and go back to your hotel room." She suggested. "I'd like to talk to your room mate too and maybe they didn't see us so they won't know to look for me there.

"Have they followed you like this for the entire time you've been in Guam?" Raven asked as they started to walk.

"No. I remained undetected for a while but about a year and a half ago I began to suspect several of the members of the local police department and when I started asking questions I started having company all the time."

"What made you suspect cops?"

"Several things." Peaks explained. "One, the killer has never been caught. Two, when my chief asked for the case files the department didn't give up all the files. I got in and had a look at what they had about six months ago and there was a whole lot of information that had been left out. Anyone could look at those files and establish a link between the murders but the police here haven't. I had to ask myself, why not. Unless..."

"Unless the police were covering something up." Raven finished.

"Right." Peaks confirmed. They reached the store and Peaks had the clerk call them a cab. When the cab arrived Raven gave the name of the hotel and they both sat back making small talk. As far as the cabby was concerned they were just tourist. Once at the hotel Peaks hopped out and opened Raven's door to help her out.

"Thank you." Raven said accepting her hand. They went into the hotel and Raven checked with the clerk, a young man, to see if Johni had gotten her message. The clerk confirmed that she had and that according to the last clerks notes she had gotten the message about an hour and a half ago.

"Did she leave the hotel?" Raven asked perplexed. If it had been that long ago that she had received the message Johni should have been at Roma's.

"I don't know Ms. Michaels." The clerk said. "I just came on duty." Raven thanked him and lead the way to the elevator. Worry was setting in and it must have been obvious to Peaks because she remained quiet. Once upstairs she lead the way to their room. As they approached the door they both could see that it was ajar. Peaks put a hand on Raven's arm to stop her.

"Let me go first." She whispered. Peaks produced a gun from behind her. Raven hadn't noticed a gun before. She stepped back respectively and let Peaks take the lead. Peaks edged up to the door and stopped. She appeared to be listening. Raven strained to do the same. Her insides were screaming, run in and call Johni's name but she forced herself to be calm. Something was wrong though, she could feel it. Peaks edged a little closer to the door and motioned for Raven to get against the door. Raven did as she was told. Peaks waited a couple of seconds and then burst through the door gun leveled. Raven stayed behind her looking around desperately for some sign of Johni. There were none. The room was in shambles. All of their possessions were thrown about the room. The drawers and closets had been emptied. Even the mattresses had been lifted and then set back haphazardly. In the bathroom everything had been dumped out of their cases and a lot of her makeup was in pieces. Peaks checked all of the rooms and the balcony. Raven searched for a note, something, anything that would tell her where Johni was. Peaks walked over and closed the door to the room. Raven sat down on a chair fighting tears of fear.

"Where is she Grady?" Raven asked knowing Peaks had no more idea then she did. Grady Peaks surveyed the room setting a hand on Raven's shoulder.

"I don't know Raven but we'll find her." She assured her. "I promise."

Chapter 19

Johni opened her eyes. Her head felt groggy and the pounding in her ears was almost deafening.

"Where am I?" She whispered. Looking around it all started to flood back, the taxi, the dark parking lot and the cloth placed over her face. She'd been kidnapped. Forcing herself to relax Johni took stock of her situation. She was sitting in a high back chair. Her feet were tied to the front legs of the chair and her hands were tied behind her back. She struggled for a moment with her bonds and when they wouldn't budge she relaxed again. There was no use in wasting energy. She surveyed the room. It was large and dark, a warehouse of some sort. Johni concentrated on adjusting her eyes as much as she could. In front of her were several large crates with no identifying marks. To her left she could make out a door. The windows that she could see, three of them, were high up almost to the ceiling itself. An exhaust fan sat idle on the left hand wall. From where she was sitting the only way out was the door. She listened for sounds, there were none.

"Well you've gotten yourself into a mess." She said out loud while she again tried to work the bonds. They were tight.

"Think Andrews." She said loudly, "Think!" Raven was out there by herself and she couldn't afford to be sitting here doing nothing. She moved in the chair as much as the ropes on her wrists would allow. If she really contorted herself she could turn slightly to the side. Now, she thought excitedly, if I can just loosen the ropes enough to get to my pocket. Whoever was responsible for her being here hadn't bothered to empty her pockets and thanks to her morning ritual, her pocket knife lay securely where she tucked it, in the upper part of her right pocket. It had a small clip which allowed her to hang it just inside of the back corner so she would have to dig into the pocket. Seeing a course of action Johni began to methodically work the ropes on her wrists.

* * *

Raven sat staring at the mess that had once been their room. Peaks was on the phone and Raven had intended to pick up what she could but she sat instead not able to stop crying. Johni was in trouble and she felt helpless. They had decided not to call the police. Since Peaks felt that someone on the force might be the killer it was obviously not an option but Peaks said she knew someone they could trust. She was talking to whoever that person was now but Raven couldn't bring herself to listen, her stomach ached. Where was Johni? Was she okay? Was she still alive? As Raven sat and ran the possibilities through her mind she went from pained to angry. Who would do this and why would they want Johni? As Peaks hung up the phone Raven stood with a renewed sense of urgency.

"What did they say?" She demanded as Peaks turned to her. Peaks looked at her admiringly.

"Nothing." Peaks said surveying the room again. "He's heard nothing on the streets."

"Nothing?!" Raven said loudly. "What do you mean nothing?" Peaks put her hands up defensively.

"Hey, hold up. We'll find her. Calm down."

"Calm down?" Raven questioned stepping closer to Peaks. "What do you mean calm down? It's not your woman who's God knows where, maybe even hurt!"

"Raven, we'll find her." Peaks tried to reassure her, "But we have to keep our heads, now calm down." Raven stormed out to the balcony. She knew that Peaks was right but she was still angry. After taking a few minutes to get herself together she rejoined Peaks in the room. She was on her knees surveying the floor.

"What are you looking for?" Raven asked joining her on the floor.

"I'm not sure." Peaks answered scanning the area around her. "Sometimes if you don't have anything specific in your mind it's easier for a clue to jump out at you." A knock at the door made them both jump up. Peaks pulled out her gun and Raven followed her to the door. Peaks motioned for her to ask who it was.

"Who is it?" Raven asked through the door.

"Bell hop." Peaks nodded to Raven.

"What do you need?" Raven inquired as calmly as she could.

"I have a message for Ms. Michaels." The man proclaiming to be a bell hop answered. Raven looked to Peaks for their next move. Peaks stepped to her and whispered into her ear. Raven was momentarily aware of Peaks hot breath on her.

"Tell him to put it under the door because you're not dressed." Raven cleared her voice and repeated the suggested line to the door.

"Okay." The bell hop said with a just a hint of disappointment in his voice. Raven was certain he was expecting a good tip. Johni need be in a hotel for one day before she would gain the reputation for good tips. A slip of paper came through under the door. Raven fished into her pocket and brought out a five. She slid it under the door.

"Here you go." She called. The five disappeared the rest of the way under the door and the bell hop said thanks. When she stood back up Peaks was giving her a whimsical look. Raven smiled and took the note from her. She found a place to sit before opening the paper. Peaks sat down with her. Raven looked at Peaks and breathed in slowly while opening the note. She almost dropped it when she read it.

"If you ever want to see your girlfriend again come to the Leap at midnight. Come alone and tell no one. If I see anyone else Andrews is dead and then I come for you!"

The note was made up of letters cut out of what appeared to be a newspaper. Raven handed the note to Peaks and fought back the tears again.

"So the killer does have her." She stated out loud.

"So it would appear." Peaks confirmed. They sat in silence for a few moments and finally unable to sit still any longer Raven stood up.

"I'm going to meet him."

"I can't let you do that." Peaks said calmly. Raven looked at her with disbelief.

"Excuse me?" Raven laughed sarcastically. "Who the hell are you to tell me what you can let me do?"

"Raven, this is a federal investigation and I..." Peaks started to explain but Raven put a hand up and stopped her in mid-sentence.

"I don't give a shit what it is! I have a hell of a lot more at stake here and I'll be damned if you or anyone else is going to tell me what I can and can't do!" Raven stated. She was fighting to control the level of her voice but she was on the edge of losing it.

"You could get hurt." Peaks offered weakly. She

obviously was only going through the motions of this conversation; she already realized that Raven was not going to back down.

"And?!" Raven asked. Peaks put her hands up defensively.

"Okay, okay, but I'm going with you."

"You read the note Grady. It said no one but me." Raven said heading for the bathroom. She had the urge to pee and she knew she'd better go now.

"Raven, I'm an FBI agent." Peaks argued through the bathroom door. "I'm trained to do this." Raven finished using the bathroom and looked around. What she needed wasn't in here. She opened the bathroom door to find Peaks sitting on the edge of the upturned mattress.

"Okay Grady," Raven answered, "you're right. I shouldn't go alone." Raven walked past Peaks. She found what she was looking for on the floor by the TV. She picked up the bottle of champagne she and Johni had brought back from the Falls. They hadn't even had a chance to pen it yet. She turned back to Peaks. The clock on the night stand behind her read 10:37pm. Peaks looked at her questioning.

"I'm way too keyed up," Raven offered. "Just one glass will help." Peaks nodded and stood up.

"Where are the glasses?" Raven looked around.

"In the bathroom I think." She offered.

"I'll get them." Peaks said going into the bathroom. Raven moved quickly stepping up behind Peaks and bringing the bottle down on the back of her head with a crash. Peaks sunk to the floor covered in champagne. Raven took a moment to check to make sure that she wasn't seriously hurt. She wasn't but she was out like a light.

"Sorry Grady," Raven whispered putting Peaks in a more comfortable position. "I can't let you screw this up. There's too much at stake." She took a moment to put a pillow under Peak's head. "I'll make this up to you I promise." She said standing up. With one more glance around Raven grabbed her bag and left the room.

Chapter 20

Raven sat in the back of the cab fighting fear. What the hell am I thinking, she admonished herself quietly. She had clubbed the only friend she had on the island and she couldn't trust the police. She was completely alone. It was not a good feeling. It didn't matter; the only thing that mattered was Johni. She looked at her watch 11:55p.m. The cab was probably only two minutes from the Leap. Two minutes, hardly time to think let alone time to plan.

* * *

Johni worked diligently at the bounds on her hands. She was about to give up and try something else when she felt them give. Contorting her body as best she could she reached with her fingers for her pocket. She worked slowly in case the bounds tightened from the movement. After several tries from different angles she finally felt the knife with the tip of her fingers. Trying to control her excitement Johni strained to get her thumb and forefinger on the end of the knife. She finally got a good hold on it and carefully slipped it from her pocket. Once in her hand she opened the knife and immediately went to work on the rope around her wrists. Thankfully the ropes weren't thick. She sawed on them for a few minutes and then stopped, listening for any movement. It would be worthless to cut the ropes only to be caught by whoever was responsible for her being here in the first place. After about ten minutes she felt the first layer of rope give. The rope was roughly three maybe four layers thick. She breathed in deeply before starting on the next layer.

"Come on girl," she whispered in the darkness. "Raven's waiting."

* * *

Raven got out of the cab and handed the driver the fare.

"Are you sure you want out here Lady?" The driver asked looking. Raven glanced around too. It was a dark night but the moon had risen and it's light illuminated everything it touched. Under any other circumstances it would have been beautiful. She had asked the driver to let her out about a quarter of a mile down the road from the Leap. She had reasoned on the way in that this would be a better move then allowing the cab to drop her off making her that much more assessable to the killer.

"Yes," she assured the driver. "I'm sure."

"Okay." The driver said sarcastically. "It's your money. Don't let the jungle spirits get you." With that he drove up the road a ways and turned coming back down the hill. He drove by her slowly with a look of concern on his face. Raven wondered if he was thinking that she might be headed up the hill to jump from the Leap. She waved giving him a reassuring smile. He waved back and then drove on down the hill. Raven stood for a moment watching the tail lights disappear. The island spirits, he had said. She laughed tiredly. The island spirits were the least of her worries right now. She turned and looked up the hill. In the dim moonlight she could make out the gate that led to the Leap, it stood ominously open, beckoning her to come ahead.

* * *

Johni worked through the last layer on the ropes. She was sweating profusely now and beads of sweat were rolling into her eyes and making them burn. She had been wrong in her initial estimation of the rope. There had been seven layers, not three or four. Her wrists hurt now from the twisting motion it was taking to cut the ropes. She felt moisture on her left wrist and she was pretty sure it was blood. It stung. She felt the last layer start to give way and excitement ceased her body. Working faster now spurred on by the thought of freedom Johni sawed at the ropes faster. It was about to give when a noise made her stop. She tried to control her breathing and calm the fear the noises had brought her. She strained to listen. She heard the slam of a car door. Someone was here. Damn, she thought, I was almost done. She settled back into the chair and hung her head a little. She wanted to appear groggy. A door opened and she fought the urge to look up. Footsteps came out of the dark. She heard the click of a lighter and saw a faint glow on the floor in front of her. She looked up lifting her head slowly. She first caught sight of a pair of legs and as she lifted her eyes further she realized that the person standing in front of her was a woman. She let her head drop as if she were still a little out of it. She heard a chuckle as the woman turned and disappeared into the dark. Johni lifted her head again this time with a touch more strength. She watched in the dimly lit room as the woman who's face she could not make out pulled a chair from against the wall and dragged it to the edge of the light that encircled Johni. She sat down and Johni could tell that she was being surveyed.

"Who are you?" Johni croaked. Her throat was dry. Silence followed her question. "Who are you?" She repeated. The other woman got up and disappeared into the darkness one more time. She returned with what appeared to be a glass of water.

"How do I know it's not poisoned?" Johni spat as the water was offered to her. Her captor laughed and held the water to Johni's lips. Johni sipped it carefully. She didn't taste anything but water. She took on more sip and then leaned back to indicate she'd had enough. She looked up at the woman with the glass. Where had she seen her before? As the woman turned and set the glass down by her chair realization hit Johni like a brick.

"You're that woman who was talking to Raven at Tanners party." Johni stated.

"Bingo." The other woman chimed.

"Rona," Johni said putting a name with the face.

"Right again." Rona said retaking her chair. She pulled it forward slightly so that Johni could see her face. "I suppose I owe you a brownie button."

"Why am I here?" Johni demanded. Rona smiled and rocked back in her chair a little. Johni could hear her grandmother in the back of her mind saying, don't do that you'll fall backwards.

"Look at it as a sacrifice for your community."

"Excuse me?" Johni asked carefully. "I don't think I understand." Her captor favored her with a look of amusement. Johni felt anger welling up inside her. "Why would a Lesbian want to kill other Lesbians?" She demanded. Johni was tired of the games. Rona looked around as if to make sure they were alone. After a moment she appeared satisfied and leaned forward slightly.

"I guess there's no harm in telling you." Rona said smugly. Johni pulled at her wrists a little, the ropes were on the verge of giving.

"I think it's the least you can do if you're going to kill me." Johni said sarcastically. Rona laughed.

"I'm not going to kill you. You're going to kill

yourself."

"I'm sure I'll have some help."

"Everybody needs help now and again." Rona responded with a laugh. Johni glared at her captor.

"Why are you doing this?" She asked again with a little more impatience. She was wasting time; she needed to get to Raven.

"Why am I doing this?" Rona asked repeating Johni's question. "I'm not doing this. I'm merely a worker. A drone if you will." Despite the current situation curiosity got the best of Johni.

"What are you talking about?" Johni asked carefully.

"I told you. You're helping your community with the sacrifice of your life. Yours and that of your girlfriend." The mention of Raven brought fear back to Johni.

"My girlfriend?" Johni said in a panic. "What are you talking about? I'll kill you if you've harmed her!" Rona put up a hand.

"She's not dead." She offered looking at her watch. "At least not yet." Time. Johni thought to herself. There isn't much time. She did her best to calm herself. She had to get Rona to tell her where Raven was.

"Where is she?" Johni asked evenly.

"She's meeting some friends." Rona said impatiently. "If I were you I'd concern myself with my own situation."

"And what is my situation Rona?" Johni asked

carefully. Rona fell silent. Johni pushed further. "If I'm going to be sacrificed I should know why." Her captor seemed to consider this for a moment.

"You're right." She stated frankly. "But I told you, it's for your community."

"I don't understand." Johni said calmly. "I thought that by getting married I'd be helping my community." Rona let out a bellow of a laugh.

"That's what they all think but they don't know. They don't have all the facts."

"What don't I know Rona?" Johni said trying to mock plead. It must have worked because Rona looked as if she suddenly felt sorry for Johni.

"The government," Rona stated plainly as if this should mean something to Johni. When Johni looked confused Rona continued. "This whole ploy to legalize gay and lesbian marriages is a push to destroy our community." Johni had to fight laughing.

"Where did you get an idea like that?" She asked carefully trying desperately to keep the amusement out of her voice.

"We know." Rona stated flatly. "We've seen the papers and spoken to those who know." The look in Rona's eyes made Johni's blood run cold. She believes this, Johni thought to herself. And the sound in her voice, it was...strange. She pushed on.

"Rona, who have you spoken to?"

"There's an operation to legalize gay and lesbian marriages but it's not from gays and lesbians it's from the government. They plan to legalize it and offer us a community of our own. When it's all done they are going to kill us." Johni fought the urge to stand and slap Rona back into reality.

"Rona," she said carefully, "how are they going to do this?" Rona looked away for a second and then back to Johni. When she answered her voice was flat.

"They are going to offer to let us all live here and on other islands and when we do they'll gas us like they did in Germany to the Jews."

"What?!" Johni asked shocked.

"It's true. An agent from the government who was against the plan came here to warn us. The bill that legalizes the marriages here and in Hawaii is the catalyst. The Sisterhood has to stop it."

"By killing our own people?" Johni asked incredulously. Rona nodded slowly.

"We have to give the illusion that it's dangerous. Ni...," Rona stopped and considered before continuing, "Our leader has determined that the best way to do this is to show the heterosexual society that lesbians are unstable."

"And your leader is it a man?"

"No, she too is a lesbian, that's why we know she has

the best interests of the community in mind. At first some of us were unsure but after a time we came to realize that it's for the best." Rona explained. This whole thing was beginning to sound a little cult-ish. Johni pushed on.

"Rona don't you think that it would be bold of the government to try and wipe out a lot of people like that?"

"No." Rona stated. Johni explored Rona's eyes. She had adopted a faraway look and her voice had remained flat. Johni decided to try something she learned while researching hypnotism for one of her novels.

"Rona," she said in an even voice. "Do you know what year it is?"

"1997."

"Rona, do you know who you are?"

"Rona Duncan." Rona's voice was flat.

"Rona, bark." Johni said in the same even voice.

"Bark!" Rona responded flatly. Excitement welled up once again within Johni. Rona had been hypnotized. No wonder she was spouting all that garbage about the government.

"Rona," Johni said again.

"Yes?"

"Rona, where's Raven?" Johni asked the question and then held her breath.

"On the Leap," Rona answered. Johni's heart almost stopped. She had to be careful now.

"Rona, who's she with?" Rona hesitated. Johni quickly asked another question.

"Rona, did the others who sacrificed do so on their own?"

"Yes."

"Rona did someone talk to them before they sacrificed?"

"Yes."

"Rona, did they talk to the leader?"

"Yes."

"Rona, what is the leader called?"

"Shazta."

"Rona does Shazta talk to you like I am?"

"Yes." Johni took a moment to breathe. It was clear now that this Shazta was hypnotizing people. It certainly explained why the police never found any signs of struggle. Whoever this Shazta was they were obviously hypnotizing people to leap to their deaths. It also explained how someone could get Ricki, who was afraid of heights up to the Leap.

"Rona, where is Raven?"

"The Leap,"Rona responded flatly.

"Rona, who is she with?" Again Rona hesitated and then with an obvious effort she blurted out the answer Johni did not want to hear.

"Shazta."

Chapter 21

Raven stepped to through the gate that allowed entrance to The Leap. She didn't have a plan. Not really anyway. Find Johni was as far as she got. It was difficult to plan when she had no idea who she would be meeting. She stepped to the right of the gate choosing to follow the line of trees in that direction. The Leap area was beautiful. In the distance she could hear the waves crashing against the rocks below the cliffs. She had the sudden flash of Ricki's broken body at the foot of the Leap and it spurred her on. It was dark but the moonlight provided enough light to navigate by and see for a short distance. She scanned the area. She saw no one. Continuing along the tree line Raven surveyed the area for possible escape routes. There was a public bathroom in the small park area that preceded the Leap and the sectioned off scenic area. The island park services had erected a protective railing on the Leap Point where you could stand and look over the edge of the cliffs or out over the village of Agana. Judging from the pictures she's seen view was incredible. After Ricki's untimely death from this spot Johni wouldn't bring her up here and Raven understood. Raven made her way to a spot that was maybe ten feet from the actual Point itself. She still saw no one. On the point she could see the railing and a bench provided for those who wanted to rest their feet while watching the sun set over the bay. She edged her way to the point watching all the while for any signs of life nearby. She felt drawn to the Point. The crashing of the waves was louder now and she started to shiver slightly. It wasn't a cold shivering but the kind of shivers one would get from knowing they were spending the night in a house where someone was killed. With one last glance at the park area for movement Raven walked quickly to the Point and grabbed the rail tightly. She looked out over the cliffs. She experienced an involuntary intake of breath as she scanned the horizon. The night sky was clear and extraordinary. There were stars for miles and so many that it was almost impossible to finds a spot that was void of them. The waves could be heard rolling in and plummeting the rocks below. There was a breeze that tasted of salt and flowed warmly around her. To her left were the lights of the village. Agana was bigger then she'd first thought. The lights were spread out though not bunched together like those of a city on the mainland. Raven marveled at how peaceful it was here. It was hard to imagine that a place like this would reek of such tragedy. She enjoyed the scenery for a few more minutes. She was about to turn to leave when she took one more look over the edge. Her heart suddenly went out to Ricki again.

"It's a long way down." Came a voice from behind her. Raven jumped and let out a small cry. She wheeled around to see who was behind her. She was shocked to discover Nicole Tanner standing just off the Point. Could Nicole be the killer?

"What are you doing here?" Raven blurted out trying to control her fear.

"Meeting you," Nicole answered casually. She stepped up on the Point and sat down on the bench. She ceremoniously crossed her legs and folded her hands on her lap.

"Where's Johni?" Raven asked carefully looking around for signs of anyone else.

"She's not here." Tanner said flatly. Raven didn't like the look in her eyes.

"Your note said to come if I wanted to see her."

"Not to worry," Tanner said glancing out over the water. "She'll be joining you." Raven didn't like the way that sounded.

"What's going on Nicole? Raven asked. She had to buy some time, figure out what to do next.

"You're going to make a sacrifice for the good of your people." Tanner responded flatly.

"Meaning?" Raven pushed. If she were going to die she certainly wanted to know why. Tanner laughed.

"I guess there is no harm in telling you. It might help me deal with some of it to talk." Tanner looked down at her hands and then back at Raven. Great, Raven thought, so now I'm hearing confessions.

"Go ahead." Raven said leaning against the rail. She made a point to hold onto it tightly.

"It all started several years ago when I fell in love for the first time in my life." Tanner started. "I had been with roughly eight women throughout my adult life and none of the relationships worked out. Every woman I'd met and felt anything for was controlling. They all wanted to tell me what to do and how to do it. I hated it. My heart ached for a person in my life that I could be with who wasn't interested in controlling me, who would just love me for who I was. I had all but decided to never indulge in another relationship when I met a man who told me that I could get women to do anything I wanted. He told me of how he had learned a skill that had allowed him to get whatever he wanted or needed from a relationship. He was talking about hypnotism. At first I didn't believe him but he took me out one night and showed me how it worked. We went into a noisy crowded bar and he did it right there. He had this woman doing exactly what he wanted. I was amazed. I begged him to teach me how. He said he would but he wanted something in return. I wanted to learn so badly that I told him I'd do anything. He agreed and taught me what I had wanted to learn. It didn't take long for me to learn and to be honest I had some sort of a natural gift for it. Before long I had women doing everything I wanted. I was really enjoying my new found talent when my teacher decided to call in his marks. He had taught me and now he wanted his favor. He explained to me what he wanted and I agreed. It didn't seem like much at the time." Tanner stopped for a moment to take a breath. Raven took the opportunity to glance around for help again. Tanner caught her looking and smiled.

"There's no one here but us Raven so you can relax."

"You were saying," Raven prompted.

"Oh, yes, where was I? Anyway, what he wanted was to be able to speak at a lesbian bar in Agat. He was an island official and he explained to me that he had been trying to speak in this bar for some time about safety and that the women wouldn't let him in. He knew that I was politically active and wanted me to set it up. It seemed harmless enough so I did it. I had no idea at the time what he really had in mind." For the first time since she had started speaking Raven saw sadness and regret in Tanners eyes. She nodded for her to continue. "I set it up and on the night he was to speak I even introduced him to the crowd. They listened to what he had to say and that was that. At least I had thought so. After he spoke he bought a round for everyone in the bar. Of course a cheer always goes up for whoever is buying so he actually ended up winning some people over. That night I used what he taught me to get the attentions of a young woman in the bar. I left with her about nine that evening. When I left he was having a good time talking to some people. When I brought the young lady I had left with back to get her car the next morning the place had been burned to the ground. I was shocked. The rumors were that it had been done on purpose and that the exits had been blocked. At first I thought that my friend had died too but later that day I discovered that he hadn't. I called him to find out what had happened and he asked me to meet him up here. I met him and what he told me next changed my whole life." Tanner stopped speaking and got up. Raven readied herself. Tanner walked to the railing and put on foot on the bottom bar. When she spoke again it was apparent that she was crying.

"He told me that he had done it. He had killed all of those people in that bar." Tanner stopped again and her words hung in the air. "He had done it and I had helped him."

"You didn't know though." Raven offered. She was feeling a small tug at her heart but quickly squelched it.

"No, I didn't but I still had a hand in it. He told me that if I said anything he'd tell the authorities that I'd helped. He would have proof; after all I did set the whole thing up. A lot of people saw he and I hanging out together, he said he would do it and I believed him." Raven looked over the side of the rail and a thought occurred to her.

"That's why there's never a struggle, the suicide

victims are hypnotized."

"Yes." Tanner said quietly. "You would be amazed at how easily it's done."

"Did you kill the others?"

"No." Tanner answered simply. "He did."

"I don't understand," Raven said perplexed. "Why are you doing this now if you really didn't have anything to do with what happened at the bar?"

"I have to." Tanner said sadly.

"But why?" Raven asked.

"If I don't he'll kill me like he did the others."

"You mean to tell me that this guy has been killing people all of this time and you've said nothing? How could you do that? How could you let him kill your own people?" Raven asked anger seeping into her voice.

"You don't understand. He can do things. He can make other people do things." Tanner whined. "Hell he even has the others believing that what we are doing is for our own good!"

"What?!" Raven said with surprise. "What others?" This was getting worse with every sentence. Tanner rushed to Raven's side before Raven could react.

"Seven, they call themselves the Sisterhood and they bow to his every demand." Tanner explained in a hurried whisper. "They believe that the government wants to legalize gay marriages so that they can put us on an island

and kill us. He had them hypnotized, under his control. I'm telling you the man is dangerous."

"Why don't you go to the authorities?" Raven demanded.

"I can't!" Tanner shouted. She was afraid it was obvious but Raven could see that convincing her to go for help was going to be difficult. Whatever this man was doing he had a strong hold on Nicole Tanner. Tanner stepped back and suddenly there was a gun in her hand. Raven hadn't even seen her reach for it.

"Nicole, I can help you." Raven said carefully. "You don't have to do this."

"Yes I do." Tanner said raising the gun.

"Nicole we can go to the authorities. We can get help." Raven pleaded. Tanner started to cry.

"You don't understand." Tanner wailed pitifully. She leveled the gun off and put her finger on the trigger. Raven felt her knees get weak. Oh Lord, she thought to herself, don't let me go out like this. She closed her eyes and heard a gunshot. Her body jerked involuntarily. She waited for the pain but there was none. She opened her eyes in time to see Nicole Tanner slip to the ground. She did a quick check of her own body and then went to Nicole's side. She fell to her knees. Tanner was breathing in short labored breaths. She was dying. Raven looked up to see Grady Peaks appear from behind the public restroom.

"Where's Johni?" Raven asked the dying woman.

"I...don't....know....."

"Why didn't you go to the police?" Raven asked her again

"He......was...... police." Tanner rasped. She watched as Nicole Tanner took her last breath. She reached out and closed the woman's eyelids. Tears welled up. When she stood up Peaks was beside her.

"Where's Johni?"

"I don't know." Raven said tears flowing freely. Peaks put an arm around her.

"We'll find her." She assured Raven.

"I wouldn't be so sure," came a voice out of the darkness. Peaks raised her gun swinging it from side to side while she shoved Raven behind her. "That's not going to do you any good Peaks." The voice stated. "Put the gun down." Raven tried to follow the voice.

"Now Peaks or Ms. Michaels dies right there beside you." Raven traced the voice to a group of trees several yards away. It was a man. She was sure that it was the man Nicole had spoken of. She looked at Peaks and nodded. Peaks slowly put her gun down.

"All right then," Peaks shouted. "I'm putting it down. Show yourself." The figure stepped from behind the trees. It was indeed a man but in the dark Raven couldn't see his face. Something about the voice was familiar.

"Where's Andrews?" Peaks asked loudly.

"Dead," the man answered flatly. Raven felt her stomach drop. Dead? She asked herself, did he say dead?

"I don't believe you!" Raven shouted. The man laughed and threw something in their direction. It landed at Raven's feet. She bent to pick it up and was shocked to find that it was the small silver and turquoise Indian arrow Johni always wore around her neck. She had given it to her shortly after they'd first met and Johni never took it off. She wouldn't even let the doctors take it off when she was in the hospital a few years back. Tears streamed down Raven's face. Absently she shook her head.

"NO!" Raven screamed at the man. She started forward but Peaks grabbed her. She collapsed into Grady Peak's arms. "No." She wailed again. She cried openly now. Peaks held onto her trying to comfort her. She cried heavily for several more minutes and then she felt anger seeping into her heart. She stood up stubbornly, surprising Peaks. The man still stood just out of the light.

"Show yourself, you chicken shit!" Raven shouted. "I want to see the face of the man I am going to kill." The man laughed but stepped into the light. Raven was shocked as was Peaks. The moon illuminated the face of Paul Greyson, Detective First Class of the Guam Police Department.

"I don't believe that you are in any position to kill

anyone Ms. Michaels." Greyson offered. In his hand he held his police revolver.

"I don't understand." Raven started. "You were the head of the investigation, you asked us to help."

"Of course I did." Greyson answered. "What better way to control you. You surprised me though Ms. Michaels. People were responding to you and you were making friends with my people. If I had left you alone you would have figured it out."

"But why encourage us?"

"My mistake," Greyson said causally. "I had tired of how easy it had all become. I thought you'd present a small challenge. I under estimated you though and then I found out about Peaks here and well I could have the three of you wandering around now could I."

"Nicole told me the whole story." Raven stated matter of fact.

"And?" Greyson asked. He had a point, Raven decided. She decided to buy them some time. Maybe that cabby would get curious after all.

"Why?" Raven asked carefully. She felt Peaks shifting from one foot to the other.

"Revenge what else."

"What happened Greyson?" Peaks piped off. "Lose your wife to a dike?" Greyson leveled his gun and popped off a round just shy of Peaks who ducked quickly.

"Remember who is in charge." Greyson demanded. Raven spoke quickly to defuse the situation.

"You had to have a reason." She stated. "If you're going to kill us we deserve to know that truth." Greyson considered for a moment.

"My sister came to Guam in 1976." Greyson started. "She was in the Air Force. She had chosen to come here because I had told her what a great place it was. I myself had been station here with the Navy and was planning to come here to settle within the year when my duty was over." Adrienne was here six months when my parents received a letter from her telling them she was getting out of the service and staying on Guam. Since I was coming back myself I was excited that my baby sister had decided to stay." Greyson stopped talking and took a breath. He started pacing when he continued. "I arrived as scheduled and Adrienne picked me up at the airport. We had a wonderful time hanging out and she helped me find an apartment and settle in. I was here two months when I met a woman and fell in love. Her name was Elaine and she was the most exquisite woman I'd ever met. We went out a couple of times and I was going to ask her to marry me." Anger was creeping into Greyson's voice. Raven felt Peaks stiffen a little. "I had set up this whole dinner thing." Greyson continued. "I had wine, flowers the whole nine yards. I was going to go to her place pick her up, take her to dinner and ask her to be my wife. When I got to her place I knocked and no one answered. I could hear the shower so I knew she was home. I knew where she kept the spare key so I fished it out of the flower pot on the porch and let myself in. I was going to surprise her in the shower. I undressed in the living room and went to the bathroom. When I got close to the door I heard moaning. I was instantly turned on at the thought that my woman was doing herself in the shower. I opened the bathroom door and I couldn't believe what I was seeing. Elaine wasn't alone. She was in the shower with someone. Pissed I threw back the shower curtain." Greyson stopped for a minute. He was very agitated. He turned to Raven and there were tears in his eyes. "Can you believe it?!" He shouted. "She was in the shower fucking my own sister! I couldn't believe it! My sister! Well, I killed them right there! Both of em! Ripped the towel bar off the wall and beat them both to death. I could have that happen! My sister was no lesbian! When I was through I put both bodies into the car and drove up here. I threw them from the cliffs." Greyson said proudly. "Hitting all those rocks, no one would know. I went back to clean up the apartment and while I was there I found all this stuff on the local gay and lesbian community. I knew right away that's what had happened. Adrienne and Elaine were just victims of the local crazies. I knew right then and there what I'd have to do. I became eradicator."

"What did the Sisterhood have to do with this." Raven asked carefully. Greyson laughed.

"I had to appear like I had no problems with the homos and besides I needed help. I used hypnosis. I was quite a magician in the Navy you know." Greyson added proudly. "The dykes provided cover and they did the leg work for me, finding lesbians who wanted to get married. I enjoyed killing in pairs. Now, if you're quite done with you questions I have business to take care of." Peaks took a fighting stance next to Raven.

"Wait!" Raven shouted as Greyson leveled the gun again. "How are you going to explain all the bodies? You have two more then you need." Greyson smiled.

"The sharks come to this side of the island once a year. There won't be anything left to explain." Raven ran out of ideas. She reached out and took Peaks' hand.

"What now?" She asked Peaks sarcastically.

"Pray." Peaks whispered back. Greyson leveled the gun at Raven. Again she closed her eyes. She heard the shot and again she waited for the pain but instead she felt Peaks go down.

"NO!" She shouted as she dropped to her side. Peaks was bleeding from her shoulder. Raven put her had on the wound trying to stop the bleeding. She heard a commotion but was too focused on Peaks to look.

"I'm okay," Peaks whispered, "Help Johni."

"Johni?" Raven asked not comprehending. She turned to see Johni on the ground with Greyson. They were both throwing punches. As soon as it registered she was up searching for the gun Greyson had pointed at them and shot Peaks with. She searched desperately. Greyson looked as though he was getting the best of Johni. He had her against the railing now. Raven spotted the gun several feet away. She had to get to it before Greyson lifted Johni over the rail. She wouldn't lose her twice damn it! Raven reached the gun as Greyson picked Johni up.

"PUT HER DOWN!!!!" She shouted. Greyson stopped and turned to see Raven pointing the gun at him. He dropped an injured Johni to the ground and faced Raven.

"You haven't got the guts!" He said laughing as he took a step forward. Raven felt herself start to panic. She had never shot anyone before. Hitting someone with a bottle was one thing but this was different and he was no longer holding Johni. She took a step back. Greyson stopped for a moment and smiled.

"You see, Ms. Michaels. You really haven't got the guts." He stepped towards her again and Raven heard a gunshot. Greyson bucked forward and looked surprised at Raven. She watched amazed as he slipped to the ground. Raising her eyes she watched as Johni, Peak's gun in hand limped to Greyson's body. She rushed to her aid. Raven caught her as she stood over Greyson. He looked up at Johni blood running from the side of his mouth.

"Your right," she said to Greyson pulling Raven close. "She doesn't have the guts, but I do." In the distance sirens wailed.

Chapter 22

Johni stood waiting for Raven to make her appearance. As usual she was forcing her to wait an extra couple of minutes. Grady Peaks stood shifting nervously from foot to foot. Johni put a hand on her shoulder and smiled.

"It's not like it's going to be you." Johni offered. Grady smiled. Grady had saved her life in a way and she had definitely saved Raven's. For that she would always be grateful. After the incident at the Leap the FBI had come in and made the arrests of the remaining woman that had made up Greyson's group. After several hours of questioning and the retelling of the entire story Johni and Raven had been allowed to accompany Grady to the hospital where they stayed until they were sure she'd be okay. They would always remain friends.

"Guess I'm nervous for you." She whispered back. The music started and Johni straightened up. Both she and Grady looked to the door. Within a couple of seconds Raven appeared wearing the most incredible dress Johni had ever seen. As the music played on, Raven made her way down the center of two rows of roses that had been laid out on the floor to form a center aisle. Raven looked up and smiled. The Falls restaurant had been decorated to the T. The island police department finished what Greyson had started and took care of the bill. One of the local gay and lesbian clubs decorated and it looked wonderful. There were many people present and although Johni and Raven didn't know most of them they themselves had become pretty well known. When the story of Greyson and the murders broke they had been called heroes. Dionne and her family as well as Kevin and his occupied the first several rows. Both of Raven's children beamed as they watched their mother walk down the aisle. Johni had flown them in without Raven's knowledge. She had been shocked but pleased. Raven was radiate. Johni could hardly smile hard enough as she made her way to them. A local minister had agreed to marry them and one glance back told Johni that even he was impressed with how beautiful Raven was. She finally reached them and Johni took her hand. As the minister spoke Johni replayed in her mind all that they had to go through to get to this point. Her love for Raven overwhelmed her as they stood taking the vows that would entwine them for life. Raven looked up at Johni and smiled. Johni could still hardly believe she had agreed to do this. In the hospital while Johni got an inch long gash on her temple sewed up Raven had paced. After the doctor was done Raven had held onto her for a long time. When she finally let go she announced that, if Johni was still interested, she would be very happy to be her wife. Johni had been floored but happy. Now, here they stood, taking that leap into the future.

The minister addressed Johni asking her for her promises to take care of Raven. She said "I do" so fast even the minister chuckled. He then in turn asked for Raven's promises. Johni held her breath as Raven said "I do". All the formalities aside the minister gave them a chance to say something to each other before he finished. Raven turned to Johni and smiled.

"Johni, I will always love you. I know that it's taken a while for me to do this but I believe it was because you were just too good to be true. I never thought I'd ever find anyone to love me like Walker did but God has blessed me again with you. Thank you for loving me. She reached up and kissed Johni's cheek, tears in her eyes. Johni looked to the minister and took her cue to say what she wanted to say.

"Raven, I have never loved like I do with you. From the moment I first saw you I knew that I had to spend the rest of my life with you. I can't tell you what this moment means to me but I will tell you that for the rest of your life you will want for nothing. What I can't buy you with money I will give to you with my heart. I promise to love you forever Raven. Forever."

"With the power vested in me by the common wealth of Guam I now pronounce you married." The minister finished. "You may now kiss the bride." Johni grabbed Raven and kissed her with all her heart. Raven returned the kiss as the room erupted in cheers.

"I love you." Johni whispered.

"I love you too." Raven beamed.

"This is for the rest of my life lady!" Johni added as they turned to the cheering room.

"You just try and get away." Raven said hugging her tightly. "You just try."

Acknowledgments

Thank you to my many fans and readers for spending time with us in the second Raven Michaels mystery.

To my spouse, TyAnne, who kept me at the keyboard and for those nights when she understood that I needed to stay up and write.

To my publisher, Re.ad Publishing, Inc., for being there and doing the best job a publisher could. A special thanks to Amanda Barnett of Re.ad Publishing for believing in Raven and Johni.

To my Grandmother, Minnie Ellen Essman, without you I would have never become the writer I am today. It all started with that first little journal and look at me now. Your guidance was the key.

www.ingramcontent.com/pod-product-compliance
Lightning Source LLC
Chambersburg PA
CBHW070836120626
46556CB00002B/779